Other Boc

Historical Fiction:

Saul's Quest—Saul of Tarsus appeared to have an extremely bright future. He had distinguished himself as being the star pupil of Gamaliel, who was considered the outstanding first century teacher in Israel. Although still a young man, Saul had already been accepted as a member of both the Pharisees and of the Sanhedrin, the principal legislative and judicial body of Israel.

Now the Jewish high priest has given Saul the assignment of hunting down, arresting, and persecuting the men and women who claim that Jesus of Nazareth is both the Messiah and the Son of God. Saul pursued the task with his usual dedication and determination . . . until something unusual happens on the road to Damascus. Walk with Saul on his momentous journey that radically changed not only his life, but also the history of the world.

Science Fiction / Fantasy

Wizard's Gambit— Out of the thousands of planets searched by unmanned space probes, sixteen have both water and an atmosphere similar enough to Earth's to make colonization feasible. These planets have been listed as being Earth Virtual Equivalents—or EVEs.

A power struggle is developing on Eve Twelve that could have far-reaching consequences, the ripples from which could even reach and impact Earth.

Wizard's Gambit is the story of that conflict.

[Available mid 2015]

Fractured Fairy Tale:

Ronald Raygun and the Sweeping Beauty—COLE BLACK

RAYGUN might be a well respected king, but he still had a problem. Yes, it's true old King Cole had a reputation for being a merry old soul, but at the moment he was definitely not feeling particularly merry. Frustrated would be a more accurate word. Frustrated by that stubborn and obstinate son of his!

Although Crown Prince Ronald Raygun was heir apparent to the throne, it was not at all apparent who his bride—the future queen—would be. Ronald had never met a girl he liked enough to date more than a few times, much less to consider marrying. And old King Cole desperately wanted to spoil some grandchildren before he died. Luckily, King Cole can call upon the services of his Royal Attorney, Lord Shyster, who helps him find the necessary Royal Loopholes in the law that requires royalty to only marry other royalty or nobility . . .

Although this fractured fairy tale primarily satirizes the classic *Cinderella* tale, it also manages to fracture *Sleeping Beauty* and *The Princess and the Pea* . . . while also having fun with various politicians and other celebrities. But are you astute enough to catch all the hidden meanings and references?

All titles are available on Amazon.com and Kindle.

Nicodemus' Quest

Is Jesus the Messiah?

Bill Kincaid

Although *Nicodemus' Quest* is a work of fiction, most of the characters in these pages existed, and the scenes depicted have been reconstructed as accurately as possible from data available to the author at the time the book was written. Various modern English translations of the *Bible* have been used as a basis for the scenes and dialogue, though additional dialogue has been invented from the author's imagination in order to make the scenes flow more smoothly.

ISBN 13-9781490418339

Praise for *Nicodemus' Quest*

Extensive biblical, historical, geographical, archaeological and linguistic research exudes from each page. Kincaid selected this novel approach—quite literally—as a creative-yet-solid mechanism for reporting key events in Jesus' ministry, as well as his death/burial/resurrection and the launch of the church. Kincaid has created a compelling and inventive apologetic for the Christ event. It provides a splendid opportunity to share the gospel with unbelievers who love a great story but won't sit still for a Bible study.

Review by Marv Knox, Editor and Publisher
Published in *The Baptist Standard*

Bill Kincaid has learned well the art of crafting a historical novel. The novelist who is effective in this genre must be able to piece together a detailed narrative of how things might have happened without violating the actual historical circumstances on which he is embellishing. Here is a marvelously readable story that embodies the truth of Jesus the Messiah.

Dr. Paige Patterson, President
Southwestern Baptist Theological Seminary

Join Nicodemus on his quest. He was waiting for the Messiah. He was seeking the Messiah. He longed to meet the Messiah. Perhaps you can identify with Nicodemus. Haven't you been in his sandals? Haven't you, too, sought Jesus? If you haven't met the Messiah, you will by joining Bill Kincaid on the journey from the Jordan River to the cross. If you have already met the Redeemer, you will be renewed in your faith as you walk with Nicodemus. Bill tells a remarkable story that will touch your heart and strengthen your faith!

Bryan Flanagan, VP of Sales and Training
Zig Ziglar Corporation

Nicodemus' Quest balances its status as historical fiction with proven archeological and cultural facts. It brings ancient characters and places to life with its vivid descriptions. Both Christians and those who have no religious faith can enjoy this easy to read work.

Dr. John L. Brackin, CEO
Peace for Today Ministries

I thoroughly enjoyed reading *Nicodemus' Quest*. The narrative is most creative, the premise interesting and thought-provoking. How the author ties in verbatim Scripture is particularly helpful in clarifying these historical events.

Laurie Magers
Executive Assistant to Zig Ziglar
Zig Ziglar Corporation

Bill Kincaid may well become the new John Grisham of Christian fiction. *Nicodemus' Quest* is an amazing weave of scripture into a spell-binding story of a behind the scenes investigation taken on by Nicodemus and Joseph of Arimathea. Even though this is a fictional account, the fact of the matter is that it could have actually happened, which makes this book all the more fascinating! This is also great reading because of the accuracy and detail of Jewish customs presented throughout the story. Having been to Israel several times, I found myself mentally retracing many of the steps we'd taken in Jerusalem and the surrounding area. This book will leave the believer hungering to visit the Holy Land as well as presenting the seeker with rock solid evidence that Christ is truly the Messiah. It is also a great book to read in preparing for Easter.

> Rix W. Tillman, D.Min., Past President
> Southern Baptists of Texas Pastor's Conference
> Author of *Time Sequence Bible Devotions*
> And of *Pastor Survival*

Whether you're a follower of Christ or not, this story will grab your heart and, once you turn that first page, there will be no putting the book down. As you find yourself joining in Nicodemus' search for the unquestionable truth as to whether Jesus was the Messiah or just another good teacher, the reader will be reminded of our Savior's unconditional love. Get ready to be challenged and to find out once and for all, as Nicodemus did in his quest, just who this person known as "Jesus" really was. This is a great book for the Christmas season.

> Jose Garcia-Aponte
> US Army Command Sergeant Major, retired
> Wounded Warriors Program
> Founder of *Operation Giveback*

Bill Kincaid has a remarkable gift of bringing characters of the Bible to life. As a long-time student of the Bible, I appreciate his depth of knowledge of the scriptures and Jewish traditions; and having had a forty-year career in research and development, I admire his attention to detail and his attempt to explain complex questions. *Nicodemus' Quest* is an ideal book for those seeking God and who also desire critical answers. It is a book that begs to be read more than once.

> Chet Moyers, Retired Chief Engineer
> MAC/NASA Automotive & Utility Projects

Table of Contents

Dedicated to my wife, Audette V. Kincaid,
and to my good friend, James Howard,
for their help and encouragement in the long process
between initial idea and the finished product of publishing this book.

Preface
By Dr. Lynn Eckeberger

This literary work by Bill Kincaid is remarkable. You will find yourself trying to decipher the difference between actual scripture and the carefully crafted story line.

I found myself deeply into the work before I even looked up to see the time of day. A friend asked what I was reading and my reply surprised me. I said, "I'm reading scripture that has come to light in Christian fiction."

This story will help you see familiar biblical passages in a 3-D imagination. To the scriptural historian, the story reveals an acute accuracy to the customs of the day, offering explanations to the curious without stodgy, didactic lectures. To the interested reader, the story carries a delightful, multidimensional plot. To all, it is truly an entertaining experience to share with others. I found it to be joyful, educational, and entertaining. I think it's a great work and hope others will have the opportunity to enjoy it as I did.

9

A Word from the Author

The Bible emphatically teaches that there is one—and only one—God who created all things that exist. Yet, the Bible also teaches that Jesus is both God and is the son of God. How can all three statements be simultaneously true? For that matter, if Jesus is God, why was it necessary for Jesus to pray to God? When he did so, was God talking to himself? If God is eternal and Jesus is either God or the son of God, how could he die? What was the purpose? These are issues and questions many people probably have—yet they may fail to search the scriptures found in the Bible which address those issues and questions.

The matter of salvation is too important an issue to be ignored. The answers to the questions posed in the preceding paragraph as well as other issues related to them may very well determine where we will spend eternity.

In the story that follows, these issues will be explored by Nicodemus and Joseph of Arimathea, two members of the Great Sanhedrin, the Jewish high counsel at the time of Jesus' ministry—and the same body that found Jesus guilty of blasphemy and sentenced him to death, setting in motion the events that culminated in his crucifixion. As theologians and students of the Jewish Bible, Nicodemus and Joseph are also concerned with whether Jesus might be the Messiah, which means the anointed one.

Many kings and priests were anointed with oil. However, none of those kings or priests fulfilled the prophesies regarding the Messiah whom God had promised. The one who would be _the_ Anointed One would be anointed with the power and spirit of God himself. Messiah is roughly translated as _Christos_ in Greek.

Part One

Nicodemus

Nicodemus clutched his cloak around his shoulders as he shuffled through the dusty Jerusalem streets. It was mid-morning, but the air had a bit more nip to it than it normally did at that time of day. If he thought about it at all, Nicodemus probably would have described himself as a middle-aged Jewish man. Most other observers would peg his age as being somewhat older, though they might concede that he was rather spry for his age.

As he worked his way inexorably toward the temple built by King Herod the Great, Nicodemus smiled to himself as he recalled the great transformation that had been—and still was being—wrought in that structure during his lifetime. Although old King Herod had often been referred to as the king of the Jews, he hadn't actually been much of a Jew either in spiritual terms or ethnically. He had been, after all, an Edomite rather than Jewish. As a ruthless, murderous, and suspicious ruler, he had even eliminated members of his own family that he considered to be a threat to his rule. Nevertheless, he had certainly been a shrewd and cunning politician. Since Herod knew that the best way to win over the Jewish population was to enlarge and glorify the temple in which they worshiped, that is precisely what he had done.

True, King Herod's Temple was not as ornate and beautiful as the fabled Temple of Solomon, but Herod's much larger holy place permitted many more people to worship there at the same time. It was an impressive architectural structure; many of its blocks of stone weighed at least one hundred tons. Even though construction had been going on for over forty years, workmen still labored on it. The temple, located in the northeastern corner of Jerusalem, sat directly across the Tyropean Valley from the Upper City, where most of the newer and more affluent homes were located.

Nicodemus entered the temple through the Court of the Gentiles, a huge rectangular area about thirty-five acres in size. This walled but open courtyard welcomed all people—men and women, Jews and Gentiles. Only Jews were permitted to go beyond the Court of the Gentiles into the Court of Women, and only Jewish men could proceed beyond that point.

Nicodemus passed the tables where the official money changers conducted business. Since Roman coins were considered unclean or defiled, such monetary units were unacceptable for temple offerings and purchases. However, the official money changers would change all foreign coins into those of the Sanctuary...for a fee. The temple reaped substantial profits from the business because the temple officials set the exchange rate.

Here also was the market where live animals could be purchased for sacrifice in the temple. Jewish religious law required sinners to present a lamb without spot or blemish as a blood offering in order for the person's sins to be forgiven. Since such a lamb would be the best of the flock, it would be a financial as well as a literal sacrifice— and it provided several important lessons for the offender. It impressed upon the individual that sin had consequences. Since God required a blood sacrifice as atonement, it demonstrated both God's sense of justice and how seriously he viewed sin. It also graphically illustrated God's mercy, since he accepted the blood of an innocent lamb to be shed as a substitute for the sinner's own blood, even though it was the human who had sinned and therefore deserved to die.

Technically, the sinner was supposed to bring the best of his own flock as the sacrifice. However, many pilgrims and penitents came considerable distances, and many of them were not herdsmen and would have to purchase the sacrificial animal somewhere. By providing the service there in the temple, the priests made it simpler for the offender—and more profitable for themselves—since the priests rented out the space used by the sellers of animals for sacrifice.

Nicodemus did not pause to reflect on whether he thought such practices were right and proper, or even whether they glorified God. Rather, he hurried on to one of the chambers that had been set aside for the family of the former high priest, Annas, and his son-in-law, Caiaphas, the current high priest.

As he entered the chamber, Nicodemus saw about forty scribes, Sadducees, and Pharisees who—like him—were also members of the Great Sanhedrin. The Sadducees tended to be the more traditional elite Jewish religious leaders who held their positions primarily as a result of family connections; they controlled the temple and its rituals, and generally were more tolerant of foreign rule. The scribes achieved their status via hard work and by learning the Mosaic laws and scriptures, and were often regarded as rabbis or teachers. Although some of the Pharisees—such as Nicodemus—were also renowned teachers and rabbis, they tended to be especially known for their piety and adherence to scriptural or traditional teachings. They fasted at least twice a week, observed fixed daily hours of prayer, and generally controlled the synagogues throughout the land.

"I see you were able to make it after all," a tall Pharisee named Joseph said as he approached Nicodemus.

"Oh, I wouldn't miss it," Nicodemus replied. "Do you think this latest *holy man* is actually the Messiah, or is he merely another malcontent and rabble rouser?"

"I have no idea, but I am quite interested in seeing for myself and hearing with my own ears. Facts tend to be stretched when repeated too many times. My caravans and other business interests require me to stay on top of any major political developments."

"Either way, he has generated a great deal of excitement among the people," Nicodemus commented.

"Or at least among the more easily swayed publicans."

Conversation ceased as the middle-aged Caiaphas entered the chamber. His shoulders were slightly stooped, and his sharp eyes darted from person to person as he spoke. Although he did not wear the precious ceremonial robes that were reserved for important religious feast days—and which were kept by the Romans in cedar-lined closets in one of the four guard towers of the fortress of Antonia at all other times—his elaborate garments were still impressive enough to mark him as being the high priest. Caiaphas kept his naturally gray hair dyed black, and carried himself with an air of superiority.

"As most if not all of you know," Caiaphas said, "another pseudo-holy man has appeared in the Jordan River valley. As far as we can tell, he has not yet claimed to be a prophet of God, much less the Messiah. Nevertheless, we cannot be too careful. I would like as many of you as are willing to do so to go check him out. See what he has to say. What claims does he make? If he asserts that he is from God, what proof does he have? Is he educated or unlearned in scripture? If educated, find out who taught him. In other words, I want you to determine how big of a threat he might be to us."

"What if he is the promised Messiah?" a Pharisee named Simon asked.

"Then God help us all!" the high priest quipped to a scattering of laughter. "No, really," Caiaphas continued. "Although we may chafe under the rule of any foreign power, the Romans have largely given us a free rein with regard to our faith and the practice of our religion. However, they will not tolerate the rabble being constantly aroused to militant fever pitch by some new self-proclaimed Messiah who is ready to lead a rebellion. The Romans are not known for their mercy when they crack down on a rebellious people."

"Are we then being sent as an official delegation to interrogate him?" Simon asked.

"Definitely not!" responded the priest. "The Sanhedrin can only investigate a matter after official charges have been made. At this point in time, no charges have been filed. Since the Sanhedrin cannot legally originate the charges, this must be an informal delegation. You are in effect on a fact-finding mission."

"Are you going with us?" Joseph asked.

"No, I don't think that would be wise. If the high priest were to personally visit this apparition from the wilderness, people might attach more importance to him than would be appropriate."

"What approach do you suggest?" a Sadducee named Matthias asked.

"I don't really care what you do or how you go about doing it. According to the reports I have heard thus far, this baptizer is calling on people to repent and be baptized. Present yourself for baptism if you need to. Just bring me back a report on which I can rely."

*****

"One thing's for certain," Joseph commented to Nicodemus as they left Jerusalem along the Jericho road. "It won't be too hard to identify our 'unofficial delegation' among the people flocking to see this new holy man."

"You speak truly, my friend," Nicodemus chuckled as he looked at the others in their group. All the Pharisees were wearing brocade robes with the wide fringes that marked them as being *Chasidim*, pious men who followed the letter of the Mosaic Law. Their opponents had responded that they were merely *Perushim*, ones who were separated from the rest of humanity by their ritualistic requirements. The name given them by the opposition had stuck, morphing into the term *Pharisee*, the term by which they were now commonly known. The scribes and Sadducees also wore distinctive flowing robes fringed at the corners with very long tassels. Many of them also wore *phylacteries*—little leather boxlike pouches containing fragments of the laws of Moses written on tiny scrolls— tied across their foreheads or attached to the inner side of their left forearms. "Yes, our garments and bearing probably do set us apart."

"So much for melting into the crowd or appearing inconspicuous."

"Oh, well. That wasn't part of our assignment."

"Very true," Joseph responded as the Jericho road began its descent into the Jordan River Valley, which extends from the Sea of Galilee in the north to the Dead Sea in the south and is entirely below sea level.[1]

After the road reached the bottom of the valley, the crowds of people split into roughly three groups. The largest number

---

[1]The shoreline of the Dead Sea is the lowest point on the Earth's surface not covered with water. The Jordan River Valley is part of the Great Rift that extends approximately 6,000 kilometers—or 3,700 miles—from northern Syria to an area surrounding Lake Victoria in southeast Africa.

continued along the road into Jericho, which was located about a mile or so south of the site where Jericho had been when it was destroyed as the Israelites under Joshua captured Canaan over a millennium earlier.

A second and much smaller group headed toward the Jordan River to a place where they could cross over to the east bank. Nicodemus, Joseph and the other Pharisees, Sadducees and scribes comprising their unofficial delegation followed the remaining fairly sizeable crowd north along the west bank of the Jordan until they found the holy man they sought, a man called John the Baptist.

John the Baptist

In an area to the east of Jericho shortly before pouring into the Dead Sea, the Jordan River's current slowed and its waters collected in a number of small pools, many deep enough to permit an adult to be easily and safely immersed. John the Baptist, a wild-looking young man with long coal-black scraggly hair and beard, stood in one of those pools about twenty feet from the river's edge. He wore a garment of camel's hair with a leather girdle about his waist. John had just finished baptizing one man, who walked slowly back to the shore. Two other men stood next to the baptizer and awaited their turns.

"I baptize you with water," John announced with a gravelly voice as he took hold of one of the men, "but one mightier than I is coming, the strap of whose sandals I am not worthy to unfasten." As he lowered the man beneath the water and then raised him up, John continued, "He will baptize you not with water, but rather with God's Holy Spirit and with fire."

As John moved to the other man who stood beside him, he continued his discourse in a loud voice. "His winnowing fork is in his hand, and he will thoroughly clean his threshing floor. He will gather the wheat into his barn, but the chaff he will burn with unquenchable fire."

At that moment, John caught sight of some of the Sanhedrin delegation, three of whom had moved into a line of people on shore as if they wished to be baptized.

"You brood of snakes!" John exploded when he saw them. "Who warned you to flee from the wrath to come? Show by your actions that you are really and truly repenting. God expects more than mere religious dogma and pretended piety."

"How dare you speak to us like that!" Matthias responded indignantly.

"Do not think that you will be saved merely because you are a descendant of Abraham!" warned John. "Do not excuse yourself or your actions by telling yourselves that 'We have Abraham as our father.' I tell you most earnestly that God is able to turn these stones into children of Abraham. The wicked kings of Israel were also children of Abraham, but that did not save them. You must truly repent of your sins and accept God's mercy and gift of righteousness if you are to escape the coming judgment."

"Who are you to warn me about judgment?" asked Matthias. "I am a Sadducee and a member of the Great Sanhedrin."

"Do you produce good fruit for the Lord?" John replied. "Even now the axe is laid to the root of the trees. Every tree which does not bring forth good fruit will be cut down and thrown into the fire. Make certain, therefore, that the fruit you bear is good and pleasing to God, and that it brings glory to God Almighty."

"Then what should we do?" shouted someone in the crowd.

"If you have two coats, give one of them to someone who has none. If you have excess food, share it with others who are needier. If you are truly a child of God, you should help and share with your brothers and sisters."

The man at the front of the line on shore called out to John, "Master, I wish to be baptized—but I am a tax collector. What should I do?"

The Jews near the man quickly moved away from him, since they despised Jews who made large profits off their countrymen by collecting taxes for the hated Roman government.

"Do you truly repent of your sins?" John asked.

"I do."

"Have you sacrificed a lamb at the temple for your sins?"

"I have."

"Do you vow that you will never again collect more taxes than the amount appointed you by law?"

"I promise and bind myself accordingly."

"Then come forward and be baptized," John commanded.

"And what about us?" two Roman soldiers on the river bank yelled out. "What should we do?"

"Do not extort money from people by violence or bring false charges against anyone," John responded. He then added as an afterthought, "And be satisfied with your wages." The two soldiers mumbled to each other as they moved toward the back of the crowd.

After several hours, someone finally asked John if he might possibly be the Messiah. Nicodemus hunched forward to hear John's reply, for it was the question he himself had started to ask a half dozen times.

"Although I am the son of a priest, I am merely a man," John replied. "I am not the Anointed One, but am only the voice of one crying in the wilderness to prepare the way for the Lord. The one coming after me is mightier than I am. In fact, I am not worthy to touch even the hem of his garment. He will make straight the paths of the Lord, and will save his people from their sins. He is the Lamb of God who takes away the sins of the world, and who will be a blessing for the peoples of all nations."

"Interesting," murmured Nicodemus quietly to himself. "Most interesting, indeed!"

Prophecies

"How does it feel to be referred to as being part of a brood of snakes?" Joseph asked Nicodemus as they walked past the date palms and balsam trees that thrived in the irrigated land around the oasis at Jericho. Israel's Hasmonean rulers had built the elaborate irrigation system approximately two centuries earlier, allowing the area to become a lush verdant green oasis in an otherwise arid setting.

"Ah, yes. The Sacred Sect of Sanhedrin Serpents," Nicodemus responded, deeply inhaling the fragrance of balsam, from which was made the Balm of Gilead. "I don't recall having ever been called a snake before, and I certainly had not expected honored members of the Great Sanhedrin to be referred to as a brood of snakes!"

"At least John was looking at Matthias and his group when he said it."

"Well, if he limits the grouping to them, I can't say that he's necessarily wrong."

"What?" exclaimed Joseph, who was clearly startled by the remark. "I think you're right—but I still can't believe that you of all people would say such a thing."

"It was rather blunt of me, wasn't it?"

"Yes, Nicodemus. Uncharacteristically blunt. You normally are diplomatic to the extreme."

"Well, sometimes even diplomatic nerves can be rubbed raw by the pretended piety of hypocrites."

Joseph's eyebrows shot up and he glanced around hurriedly to see if anyone was close enough to hear his friend's words. "You're in a roguishly daring mood today!" he exclaimed.

"Don't worry, my friend; it will pass. I guess I just get tired of the charade sometimes."

"What charade?"

"The pretended religious piety we Pharisees exhibit for the world to see."

"I thought we are simply keeping God's commands as set forth in the law God gave to Moses," Joseph remarked.

"True, but I sometimes think we may be following the letter of the law not because that is what God commanded and we desire to please him, but rather so that we can impress other men and be honored by them."

"Give me an example," Joseph challenged.

"All right. The law says we should honor the Sabbath and keep it holy," Nicodemus answered. "God wanted us to set aside a day to remember all he has done for us, to be thankful, and to worship him. We, however, have set up dozens of rules and regulations that tell us how far we can walk on the Sabbath before it becomes work, or how we can do this or that, or other such nonsense."

"Nonsense?" Joseph asked in surprise.

"Yes, Joseph, nonsense. We have become so concerned with keeping the thousands of rules and regulations we have imposed that we may have lost sight of the reasons God gave us his laws in the first place. And the pretended piety of Matthias and his clique tends to rub me the wrong way."

"They *do* want others to know how good they are, don't they?" said Joseph.

"Yes, they take great pride in how much better they are than other people."

"Kind of like a pig taking pride in how much cleaner he is than the other pigs at a pig trough," Joseph chuckled.

"I like that analogy, Joseph!" Nicodemus commented. "Compared to other pigs, that pig might look pretty good. Compared to human standards of cleanliness, however, that pig is pretty dirty. Although we might prefer to compare our goodness to that of other people, that's not the correct standard. Unfortunately for us, God doesn't allow us to measure ourselves against the pig troughs of earth. It is God's righteousness that is the actual standard."

"Ouch!" exclaimed Joseph. "There's no way we can measure up to that!"

"That's why we bring our sin offerings, Joseph. And that's why John the Baptist calls for people to repent. What did you think of him?"

"Actually, I found him to be rather refreshing—in a wild and unfinished sort of way. Most of the preachers, prophets or self-proclaimed Messiahs who show up turn out to be frauds or scoundrels—or worse. However, this one brings a new variable into the mix: He claims he is not the Messiah, but is rather a forerunner sent to prepare the way for the Messiah. What do you make of that?"

"Well, John could be part of a conspiracy involving two or more people. He could simply be the front man for the group."

"Good point," said Joseph. "I had thought it might be a clever way for him to preach without leaving himself open to charges of sedition or treason."

"What do you mean?"

"Well, he doesn't claim that he himself is the Messiah, which could subject him to those criminal charges. You also may have noticed that he was preaching on the western side of the Jordan River."

"What difference does that make?"

"The other side of the river forms the border for Perea, where Herod Antipas could arrest John without first asking Governor Pilate's permission," Joseph said as he gestured toward a growth of tamarisk, willow and broom trees on the eastern bank of the river.

"Those are some interesting possibilities, Joseph."

The two men had reached an elevated area that offered a view of the Dead Sea stretching out to the southeast of Jericho. A few wispy clouds lingered lazily above the muted purple hills of Perea. Just southwest of Jericho was the gleaming white summer palace built by Herod the Great that included a theater and gymnasium in addition to its pools and gardens. Various pastel-colored vacation villas built by wealthy citizens of Jerusalem nestled around Herod's palace.

Joseph turned back to his friend and asked, "Do you think any of them are more than just possible? Are any of them what you really believe about John?"

"Not really, Joseph. I think it is more likely that he is precisely what he said: a forerunner who is preparing the way for someone else. Quite frankly, that's what I expect to happen before the actual Messiah appears."

"It is? Why?"

"Parts of the prophecies made by the great prophets Isaiah and Malachi indicate that before the Messiah comes, there will be a messenger who will prepare the way,[2] crying in the wilderness,

'Prepare the way for the Lord; make his paths straight.'" Nicodemus' right arm made a sweeping arc toward the barren hills that were visible above the rift through which the Jordan River flowed. "Isaiah said that 'every valley shall be filled, and every mountain and hill shall be brought low; the crooked shall be made straight, and the rough ways shall be made smooth; and all flesh shall see the salvation of the Lord.'"[3]

"So before the Messiah comes, you think there's going to be some cataclysmic event that knocks down the mountains, fills the valleys, and straightens the paths?" Joseph asked as the two men turned west and began climbing up the Jericho road toward Jerusalem.

"Not really," Nicodemus replied. "Isaiah was talking about preparing the way for the coming king by taking dirt from the top of hills to fill in the low parts between hills so that the King's Highway would be smoother and better than an unimproved pathway. If there are any cataclysmic events in the prophesy, it is probably just a figurative reference to a shuffling of the old order as God ushers in his new covenant. Remember that God has promised us more than just a Messiah; He has also promised to make a new and better covenant with us that will allow us to become a kingdom of priests with the right to go directly to the throne of God Almighty with our petitions and prayers rather than having to approach through an earthly priest. However, I have been at least halfway expecting some prophet or forerunner to show up prior to the Messiah."

"But we've been having self-proclaimed Messiahs crop up every few years—and sometimes we have several in the same year," Joseph protested. "What makes you think the time may be ripe for the real thing?"

---

[2] Mal. 3:1; Isa. 40:3.
[3] Isa. 40:3-5.

"Because of two of Daniel's prophecies. Do you remember his interpretation of King Nebuchadnezzar's dream?"[4]

"Vaguely," Joseph responded. "Do you have any idea how many years it has been since I read the scrolls of Daniel's prophecies? Wasn't that the dream about some kind of statue?"

"Yes, although Nebuchadnezzar did not initially remember his own dream. Well, that might not be quite true; he may have decided to withhold information about the dream in order to test his wise men. In any event, he knew it was so extremely troubling to him that the dream woke him up and wouldn't let him go back to sleep. He summoned his wise men—a group of advisers who were primarily magicians, enchanters, sorcerers, and astrologers—and commanded them to tell him what he had dreamed and then tell him what the dream meant.

"Of course, they couldn't do it. They needed to know his dream in order to have any chance of making an interpretation. Well, that set the old king off. He became convinced in his own mind that his *wise men* were not really all that wise if they could not perform the task he had set for them. He therefore ordered that all the wise men of Babylon be executed."

Joseph and Nicodemus sat down on a couple of rocks that littered the side of the road as they caught their breath and rested for a few minutes. Although Jerusalem was only fourteen miles from Jericho, it was also almost two-thirds of a mile above the Jordan River valley, and parts of the road between the two cities were steep enough to encourage travelers to find a place to rest.

"Daniel was one of the young men who had only recently been added to the king's body of wise men," Nicodemus continued.

---

[4] Dan. 2:1-49.

"When he found out what Nebuchadnezzar had decreed, he went to the king and asked for a little additional time so that he could interpret the king's dream. Then he and his Jewish friends who had been taken into captivity with Daniel earnestly prayed to God for the answers."

"Weren't those Jewish friends also some of the king's wise men, added about the same time as Daniel?"

"That's right," Nicodemus responded, "and they joined Daniel in the night of prayer. During the night God granted their request, and in a vision revealed both the king's dream and translated its meaning for Daniel. After giving thanks to God, Daniel then went to Arioch, the commander of the king's guard and the man in charge of carrying out the execution of Babylon's wise men. Daniel told him not to execute them, but rather to take Daniel to Nebuchadnezzar so that he could reveal God's interpretation.

"Nebuchadnezzar asked Daniel if it was true that he could recount the dream and then interpret it. Daniel modestly replied that no man could do what the king had requested—but asserted that there is a God in heaven who can and does reveal such mysteries."

Nicodemus and Joseph allowed a column of Roman soldiers to pass their location before resuming their upward trek toward Jerusalem.

"Daniel then reminded Nebuchadnezzar of what he had dreamed," Nicodemus said. "The king had dreamed about an enormous, dazzling statue that was unbelievably awesome in appearance. The head of the statue was composed of pure glistening gold, its chest and arms shiny silver, its belly and thighs an untarnished bronze, and its legs were made of iron—except that the feet contained a mixture of iron and baked clay. As the king looked at the statue, he became aware that a rock was being cut from the surrounding stone, not by human hands but rather by some supernatural power. The rock then struck the feet of the statue and smashed it. The iron, clay, bronze, silver, and gold broke into millions of pieces and blew away like chaff on a threshing floor, leaving no trace of the great and mighty statue. However, the rock that struck the statue grew into a huge mountain that filled the whole earth."

"Didn't Nebuchadnezzar confirm that Daniel had stated his dream correctly?" asked Joseph.

"Yes. The king indicated that his memory had been refreshed, and he confirmed that Daniel had correctly stated his dream. Daniel then revealed the meaning of Nebuchadnezzar's dream. He said that the God of heaven, who had given the king might, glory, dominion and power, had now revealed what was going to happen in the future. Daniel said that Nebuchadnezzar and his Babylonian Empire was the head of gold. After the Babylonian Empire had run its course, another kingdom would arise that was represented by the silver portions of the statue. Then would appear another empire represented by the bronze. Although Daniel did not spend much time on the first three kingdoms, he went into much more detail regarding the fourth empire, which would be as strong as iron. In its later years it would become a divided kingdom, with parts of it still being as strong as iron but with other parts being as brittle as baked clay."

"Was the Babylonian Empire the only one that was specifically identified?" Joseph asked.

"That's right," Nicodemus responded. "The others are not identified by name, but they aren't that hard to figure out. However, the important part of the revelation was that during the reign of that fourth great empire, the God of heaven will set up his own kingdom.

It will never be destroyed, nor will it be left to another people. It will overpower any kingdom that opposes it, but it will itself endure forever."

"And you think," mused Joseph, "that the rock that grows to fill the earth represents the coming of the promised Messiah?"

"I do," Nicodemus answered. "Remember that *Messiah* literally means *The Anointed One*. True, we anoint our kings and high priests with special anointing oil—but THE *Anointed One* will be anointed with the power and spirit of the living God. He is the fulfillment of God's covenant with Abraham, Isaac, Jacob, and David. I believe that it is through the Messiah's reign that all the peoples on earth will be blessed, just as God promised in his covenant."

"So you really think the Messiah will actually come—even after all these years? Remember, it has been over five hundred years since Daniel made his prophesies."

"Oh, I definitely believe God's word—and the prophesies of his prophets," Nicodemus replied.

"So do I," said Joseph. "But you seem to think it might happen at any time now. Why?"

"Think, man. Think. Daniel told us that the first great kingdom was the Babylonian Empire under Nebuchadnezzar. What was the empire that defeated Babylon and took its place?"

"I guess that would be the Medes and Persians under Cyrus the Great."

"Very good. And what would be the third great empire that conquered most of the known world?"

"That would probably be the Greeks under Alexander the Great."

"Excellent, Joseph."

"But why did you qualify your question?"

"What do you mean?"

"Alexander was unstoppable. His armies swept over all opposition—yet you only give him credit for conquering *most* of the known world."

"Ah, good point, Joseph, though it causes me to digress a bit from the point I was making. If you remember, Alexander was forced by his own commanders to turn back from their military campaign, since they had been away from their families for so long. Although Alexander could see an unconquered civilization on the other side of the river, he respected his commanders' wishes and agreed to turn back. Now, which empire took the place of the Greeks except in matters of language, culture and customs?"

"The Roman Empire, of course. So you think the Jewish Messiah will arrive some time during the rule of the Romans?"

"That's the only way I can make sense of Daniel's prophecy," Nicodemus replied as they rounded the curve of the southern foot of the Mount of Olives and Jerusalem came into view. As many times as he had seen the sight, seeing this view of the Holy City still gave Nicodemus a thrill. The panorama was dominated by the massive gold and white temple on top of Temple Mount. To the north and adjacent to the temple was the Roman's Antonia fortress. On the western hill of the city stood the grand palace built by Herod the Great.

Nicodemus paused to look at the city before continuing, "It should also be noted that Daniel made another prophecy specifically referring to the Anointed One or Messiah. Although that prophecy is more specific about when the Messiah will come, it only mentions a number without indicating the unit of time involved. Daniel said that there will be sixty-nine 'sevens' from the issuing of the decree to restore and rebuild Jerusalem until the Anointed One comes.[5] Seven times sixty-nine equals 483—but 483 what? If it is 483 days, weeks or months, they have already passed without being fulfilled. If, however, they are years, as seems most likely to me, it is just about time for the Anointed One to make his appearance and to be cut off, though I am not at all certain as to what Daniel meant by being cut off. However, it is very possible that the Messiah's coming could be imminent."

"You have really given me some things to think about, Nicodemus. I want to examine some manuscripts at the temple library, and I would like to meet with some other people I know to get more information. Would you be willing to visit with me again soon?"

"Certainly, my friend. It's a topic I enjoy immensely, though I don't pretend to have all the answers."

---

[5] Dan. 9:25.

Baptism

The next morning, Joseph was sitting at a table in his Jerusalem shipping office when a man entered the room.

"You wished to see me, sir?"

"Yes, Joshua. I'm glad you could come on such short notice. I have decided to pull you off your current assignment because I need your expertise elsewhere. Are you familiar with a man called John the Baptist?"

"Only by reputation; I've never met him."

"John is calling for people to repent, be baptized and prepare themselves for the coming of one who will baptize people with God's Holy Spirit and fire. I think he may be saying that God's promised Messiah will be coming soon."

"But sir," Joshua countered. "We have had `Messiahs' showing up rather regularly over the past few years. What makes this one different?"

"A person whose opinion I especially respect thinks this could be the real thing," Joseph replied. "He directed me to some prophecies by Daniel and Isaiah. After studying those scriptures, I have concluded that he is probably correct. With the types of business interests I have, it is imperative that we have maximum advance notice of anything as momentous as the coming of the Messiah."

"Very well, sir," said Joshua. "What is my assignment?"

"I want you to go to the Jordan River where John is baptizing. Watch him and listen to what he has to say. If anyone shows up who is identified by John as being either the Messiah or the mighty person of whom he has been speaking, find out all you can about that man and get me word immediately. As you can probably tell, I consider this to be a high priority assignment."

"Yes, sir," said Joshua as he left the room.

*****

Joshua melted into the crowds that surrounded John the Baptist, and watched and listened as John called for people to repent of their sins and be baptized. Although John often referred to someone who would come later who was mightier and worthier, no such person initially appeared.

After Joshua had watched for a period of time, a tall, slender young man with medium brown hair and beard came walking down the west bank of the Jordan River from the north. He carried himself with an air of confidence.

When John looked up and saw the man, he turned to the crowds and shouted, "Behold the Lamb of God who takes away the sins of the world!"

A noticeable murmuring raced through the crowd of onlookers as the realization set in that this was the man about whom John had been talking. Joshua moved closer to the "Lamb of God" as John climbed out of the river, used an old robe to partially dry himself, and greeted the man almost as if he were a long lost brother.

"Jesus, what brings you all the way from Nazareth?" John asked.

"I came to be baptized by you," Jesus responded.

"You can't be serious!" exclaimed John. "I should be baptized by you—yet you come to me? I ask people to repent of their sins and be baptized. How can you repent of sins you have not committed?"

"I understand your concern at baptizing me, John, but it must be done in order to fulfill all the requirements of righteousness."

John looked at Jesus silently for a few moments, and then nodded his head. The two men then walked out into the river. John placed one hand on Jesus' shoulder and raised his other hand above his head.

"I baptize you with water," John said, "but you will baptize believers with God's Holy Spirit. You will cleanse men of their unrighteousness, will drive out iniquity, and will give men a peace that surpasses all understanding. I now baptize you in the name of the mighty God of our forefathers who is also the father of all eternity."

Jesus bent his knees and John lowered him beneath the surface of the Jordan River, hesitated a moment, and then lifted him back to his feet.

As Jesus began to walk back toward the west bank of the river, a bright radiance seemed to float down from the clouds above and surround him. Joshua rubbed his eyes to make certain he was not dreaming or hallucinating, since it appeared to him as if the heavens had opened and the Spirit of God was descending like a giant dove.

Suddenly a voice boomed from above, "This is my beloved Son, in whom I am well pleased."

At the sound of the mighty voice, many in the crowd fell prostrate on the ground. Others sank to their knees and prayed, but a few looked around suspiciously to see what trick was being played on them.

Joshua mentally reconstructed his assignment. He had been ordered to immediately report to Joseph of Arimathea anything similar to what he had just witnessed. On the other hand, what he thought he had seen and heard seemed to defy conventional logical explanation. Joshua decided it would be prudent to interview other people who had witnessed Jesus' baptism to make certain their recollection of what they had seen and heard corresponded with his own.

Although some of the people he interviewed thought the glory of God Almighty had descended from the heavens, others thought it was merely an exceedingly brilliant shaft of sunlight that had pierced the clouds in such a way that it highlighted Jesus. However, all the people were in agreement regarding the mighty voice they had heard. Joshua took notes by applying a stylus to a set of wax tablets enclosed in leather-covered wooden frames that he carried with him for that purpose.

*****

Joshua then hurried back to Jerusalem, where he gave his report to Joseph. After listening to Joshua's account and asking a number of questions, Joseph went to the house of Nicodemus. A servant welcomed Joseph, notified Nicodemus of his presence, and then led him to an enclosed interior garden containing brightly colored flowers among various trees and shrubs. Nicodemus was reclining on a couch and beckoned Joseph to take his place on an adjoining one. As Joseph rested himself, the servant brought a pitcher of water, a basin and a towel, and began washing Joseph's feet. An assortment of finely diced fruit was placed on a table between the two men.

"How are things in Arimathea?" Nicodemus asked.

"Very well, my friend."

"And are your business ventures and caravans doing well?"

"Never better. Buying water rights from that consortium in Palmyra has worked out even better than I could have imagined. By cutting through the desert to Palmyra, my caravans can generally cut off several weeks' time, giving me a major advantage over my competitors. As a result, business has been very good. You are also looking good, my friend."

"Thank you, Joseph. The Lord has granted me sufficient income off my prior investments that I can now spend more time studying scripture."

"That's one of the reasons I wanted to meet with you today. You gave me much to think about in our conversations regarding John the Baptist and the coming Messiah. I have examined the writings of Isaiah and Daniel you referred to, and have assigned one of my most trusted investigators to mix and mingle with the crowds flocking to John's baptisms; he has just come to me with his report."

"You are taking this seriously!" Nicodemus exclaimed.

"Well, you know me: I never do anything half-heartedly—especially if it is something that could have a major impact on my business or financial investments," Joseph replied. "You might be interested in some of the developments. Earlier today the person John talked about apparently showed up to be baptized."

"Really! Who is he?"

"A man called Jesus of Nazareth."

"Nazareth, huh? Well, that could be a major objection to his being the Messiah."

"Why's that?"

"The prophet Micah indicates that the Messiah will come from Bethlehem Ephrathah.[6] In fact, that is one of the more useful prophecies for dismissing most of the men who have pretended to be the Messiah. Bethlehem is a small enough town that very few self-appointed Messiahs can pass that prophecy. If this Jesus is from

---

[6] Mic. 5:2.

Nazareth rather than Bethlehem, we can probably write him off. How old is Jesus?"

"My man said he is thirty years old."

"Thirty, eh? That could be another problem. Old King Herod the Great ordered his soldiers to kill every boy in and around Bethlehem who was two years old or younger not quite thirty years ago. His soldiers carried out their orders with merciless and ruthless precision. Even if this Jesus had been born in Bethlehem, I doubt he could have escaped Herod's purge. However, I fear that I may have allowed my curiosity to intrude on your account. Please continue with what you started to say about the baptism."

Joseph recounted Joshua's account of Jesus' baptism by John, ending with the mighty voice booming from heaven that declared, "This is my beloved Son, in whom I am well pleased."

"Hold on!" Nicodemus exclaimed. "Is your man certain of this?"

"Absolutely. Joshua saw and heard it himself, and he interviewed others who were there. All their accounts are consistent on that point."

"How reliable is Joshua?"

"Very reliable. During the eight years he has worked for me as an investigator, his information has always been true and correct. He's probably the best investigator I have."

"I had not anticipated that you would follow up as thoroughly as you have done," Nicodemus commented as he picked up a piece of melon. "Assigning a trained investigator to this cause must be rather expensive. Are you sure you wish to continue this exercise in such a fashion?"

"If the prospect of the promised Messiah's coming is as imminent as you believe it could be, it would be foolhardy of me not to commit such resources to discovering the truth."

"So you are willing to continue this degree of investigation for the time being?"

"Absolutely … unless, of course, you determine that Jesus is a fraud or I decide it is a waste of time and money."

"Although the fact that Jesus is thirty years old and from Nazareth weighs against his being the Messiah, I am not ready to write him off at this point. Do you have more than one investigator you would be willing to assign to this case?"

"Most definitely."

"Would you be willing to assign one of your men to find Jesus and follow him wherever he goes, and then assign your other man to find out more information about Jesus' background?"

"Of course. What type of information do you desire?"

"When and where was Jesus born? If he was born in Bethlehem, how did he escape Herod's purge? Is he connected in some manner to John? Also, find out any other details that might help us to determine the truth about him."

"I will do as you say and will try to find out what I can. If you have any special messages for me before I get back to you, you can leave them for me at my shipping office here in Jerusalem."

"Won't you stay for the evening meal, Joseph? If you don't feel like going back to Arimathea tonight, I can also offer you our guest bedroom."

"Many thanks, but business beckons. I must meet with some of my purchasers and caravan leaders, and I need to send out my investigators on our mission. However, I may be able to accept your generous hospitality at a later time."

When Joseph left Nicodemus' house, he made his way to his Jerusalem office and visited with Joshua, who had been waiting for him. Joseph gave Joshua the job of answering the questions

Nicodemus had posed. He was also given the assignment of first going to Capernaum, a city on the northwest shore of the Sea of Galilee, and enlisting the aid of Bartholomew, another investigator who worked for Joseph. Bartholomew was to follow Jesus wherever he went, observe him, and then report back to Joseph.

Investigations

When Bartholomew arrived in Nazareth, he discovered that Jesus had just left town with his mother, Mary, to attend a wedding celebration in Cana, another Galilean village a few miles to the northeast of Nazareth. Cana had been a military headquarters for Herod the Great during his war with the Parthians, but it was now a village of less than a thousand inhabitants. Cana was named for the reeds that grew in the nearby marshy area below the terraced slopes and orchards where figs and walnuts grew. Since Bartholomew had originally come from Cana and knew the people there, he had no problem locating the wedding feast and quietly blending in with the servants who were taking care of the guests. That way he could mix and mingle with both the servants and the guests without drawing attention to himself.

The wedding ceremony had taken place near the common well in the village square. During the festivities that followed, Mary went to her son, who was chatting with other guests, and told him, "The wedding hosts have run out of wine, which could cause them a considerable amount of embarrassment, since the wedding blessing has not yet been recited."

"Why are you telling me about it?" Jesus asked. "You know that my hour has not yet come."

"Just help them out," she responded. "That's all I ask."

Mary then turned to the servants and told them, "Do whatever he tells you to do."

Jesus looked around and saw six large stone jars that could each hold twenty to thirty gallons of water. The jars had been used that morning to carry water to the *mikveh* for the bride's ceremonial cleansing.

"Fill the jars with water," Jesus instructed the servants. When all six jars had been filled to the brim, Jesus turned to Bartholomew and told him, "Now draw some out, and take it to the master of the feast."

Bartholomew did as he was told, but trembled while carrying the water, since he worried about what punishment he might receive for bringing water instead of the wine the master of the feast would be expecting.

When the master tasted the liquid, however, he called the bridegroom and said to him, "It's the normal practice for men to serve the good wine first, and then after the guests are too drunk to notice the difference, they bring out the cheap stuff. Instead, you served good wine at first, but now are following it with really excellent wine!"

Bartholomew stifled a startled cry at the master's words. He then hurried back to the big stone jars, surreptitiously checked to see if anyone was watching, and quietly sampled a small amount from each of the six jars. Each of them now contained remarkably good wine instead of the water that had been poured into them.

Bartholomew sat on his haunches beside one of the stone jars and racked his brain. *How did this happen?* Since Bartholomew had helped draw the water from the well and fill the jars, he knew the liquid was water when it came from the well, and it was still water when it was poured into the jars. He thought it was still water when he drew it back out of the jar, but it had been transformed into wine by the time he reached the master of the feast.

How was that possible? Bartholomew had no explanation. He looked back at Jesus, who was conversing with two other men. Bartholomew felt certain that Jesus had somehow changed the water into wine. *But how?* He had not touched the water, the jars or even the cup Bartholomew had carried to the master. Still, Jesus' mother had asked him to help the hosts by providing more wine, and Jesus had issued commands to the servants. Bartholomew concluded that Jesus must possess some unusual or supernatural power, and Bartholomew would need to watch him even more closely. *Should he tell the master of the feast or some other official what had happened?* Bartholomew decided against such a course of action, since it would probably accomplish nothing other than calling attention to himself; it would be better to save his reports for his employer, Joseph of Arimathea.

*****

Meanwhile, Joshua had journeyed to Nazareth, an agricultural community on the southeast slope of the Carmel range. Indeed, an ancient watchtower on the uppermost crest of the hill offered a commanding view of the vast valley beyond. However, the location was at least six miles from the busy military and commercial routes that traversed the country. Nazareth was therefore considered to be a relatively unimportant and insignificant village.

While Joshua waited for Mary to return from Cana, he spent his time interviewing people of Nazareth about Jesus. Since he especially wanted to talk with Mary about her son but was not sure what would be the best way to approach her, he spent much time in prayer. By the time she returned from Cana, Joshua had decided that his best approach might be to go directly to Mary, explain his mission, and ask if she would be willing to talk with him.

When Mary opened the door of her house, Joshua blurted out, "Hail, Mary; the Lord is with you." He wondered to himself, *what caused me to say something like that?* A look of astonished wonder came over Mary's face as she fought for control of her emotions. She finally asked, "Who are you?"

"My name is Joshua, and I have been sent by Joseph of Arimathea to ask you a few questions, if you don't mind."

Mary closed her eyes for a few moments and appeared to be in quiet prayer. Then she opened her eyes, nodded her head, and asked Joshua to enter her house, a simple mud brick structure. The floor was hard-packed dirt mixed with clay, ash and straw so that it was as hard as the mud brick walls. A young man in his mid-twenties sat on a work bench in one corner of the room. He appeared to be staining a piece of wood.

"This is my son, James," Mary said.

"Shalom," Joshua nodded to James, who returned the salute.

Joshua looked around the room. A waist-high wood table was positioned along one wall, while a lower table was in the center of the room surrounded by three wooden chairs. Although the chairs were constructed of basic sycamore frames with woven-reed backs and seats, their precise and careful construction indicated that their maker had taken pride in their craftsmanship. Mats used as beds were stacked by a wall, as were a couple of wooden stools. A third stool was next to a goatskin churn, which indicated to Joshua that Mary may have been making curds before being interrupted by his visit. It was unusual to see so much furniture in a simple dwelling.

Noting Joshua's questioning gaze, Mary explained, "My husband was a carpenter, and made these items for us to use."

Mary offered Joshua a chair. "You are a man, then, rather than an angel?" she asked.

"Most definitely," Joshua responded. "Why do you ask?"

"The words you used when you greeted me were almost identical to the ones the Angel Gabriel used almost thirty-one years ago when he first greeted me. Since I've never told anyone other than my husband about that encounter, hearing the words again startled me."

"Please tell me about it," Joshua urged.

Again Mary closed her eyes in silent prayer. After several moments she opened her eyes, nodded her head, and smiled as she said, "All right. I think I am supposed to tell you everything. At the time I encountered the angel, I was a teenage girl living in Nazareth. Although I had been betrothed to a local apprenticed carpenter named Joseph, we were both careful to keep ourselves chaste and pure. Both of us were virgins.

"Imagine my surprise, then, when a mighty and overpowering angel appeared before me and said, 'Hail, favored one; the Lord God Almighty is with you!' As you can probably imagine, I couldn't think of what I should say or do.

"'Do not be afraid, Mary,' the angel assured me, 'for you have found favor with God. Behold, you will conceive in your womb and bear a son, and you are to call his name Jesus, for he will save his people from their sins. He will be great, and will be called the Son of the Most High. The Lord God Almighty will give to him the throne of his father David. He will reign over the house of Jacob forever, and of his kingdom there will be no end.'"

"That probably startled you, didn't it?"

"That's putting it mildly. All I could think of was how could I have a baby if I am still a virgin, and what would that do to my prospect of marrying Joseph? For that matter, would I even be allowed to live if people believed that I had had a baby out of wedlock? Moses' law makes such things punishable by death. I finally stammered, 'How can this be, since I am a virgin and have no husband?'

"'The Holy Spirit will come upon you,' said the angel, 'and the power of the Most High God—Yahweh Elohim—will overshadow you. Because the Lord God Almighty will use a part of his own Spirit to impregnate you, the Holy One who is to be born will be called the Son of God. Behold, your kinswoman Elisabeth has also conceived a son in her old age, and this is the sixth month with her who was believed to be barren. For with God, nothing is impossible.'"

"Are you telling me that the angel said you would be impregnated by God himself?" Joshua asked.

"Well, Gabriel said God would use a part of his own pure Spirit to impregnate me."

That's quite a story, Joshua thought to himself, but forced himself to blandly ask, "How did you answer him?"

"I didn't know what else to say or do—so I simply bowed my head and said, 'I am the handmaid of the Lord; let it be to me according to your word.' The angel then departed."

"What happened next?"

"I decided to see if what the angel had said was true regarding Elisabeth," Mary responded. "After all, she had always been barren and was now thought to be too old to have a baby. I therefore hurried to the house where she lived with her husband, a priest named Zacharias."

"What did you find out?"

"Well, it was true that Elisabeth was six months pregnant. When I walked into the room where she was resting, she immediately cried out, 'Blessed are you among women, and blessed is the fruit of your womb! But why am I so favored, that the mother of my Lord should come to me? As soon as I heard the sound of your greeting, the baby in my womb leaped for joy.'"

"That's a rather unusual greeting. How did she know you had agreed to be used in that manner by the Lord Almighty?"

"I think she must have been filled with God's Holy Spirit," Mary answered. "I stayed with Zacharias and Elisabeth until the time came for her to have her baby. When the official Jewish delegation gathered to circumcise her son eight days after he had been born, they wanted to call him Zacharias, after his father.

"'No,' Elisabeth answered, 'he is to be called John.'

"'None of your kin is called by that name,' they protested. The Jewish delegation then asked Zacharias what he wanted to name the boy. They handed Zacharias a writing tablet, since he had been struck mute by the angel Gabriel almost a year earlier.[7] Zacharias therefore wrote out on a tablet, 'His name is John.' Immediately, the priest regained his power of speech, and he was careful to praise God."

"Did that startle the visitors?"

"Did it ever!" Mary exclaimed. "While I was staying with Zacharias and Elisabeth, I realized that even though I was still a virgin, I was now pregnant! I also knew that I would need to explain the situation to my betrothed, Joseph."

"What was Joseph's reaction?" Joshua asked.

"As you might imagine, he was utterly shattered. Joseph said he couldn't believe that I was actually the kind of woman who would have relations with any other man after entering into a Hebrew

---

[7] Because Zacharias had not believed the angel when he told Zacharias that his barren wife was about to have a baby son. The angel had told him that they were to name the boy John.

Eyrusin betrothal. He reminded me that after we participated in the Eyrusin ceremony, we were considered married even though we continued to live separately until the end of the betrothal period.[8] We were expected to keep ourselves sexually pure throughout that time.

"Joseph seemed even more disappointed that I apparently couldn't believe in him enough to tell him the truth, and instead had invented such a far-fetched story! I ran home crying, and earnestly prayed that God would take control of the situation."

"Did you talk with Joseph again?"

"Yes. Joseph came to me the next day and told me what had happened after I had made my startling announcement. He said he had thought and prayed about the situation all day, and had finally decided to quietly divorce me rather than make a public example of me. However, that night, an angel of the Lord appeared to him in a dream and said, 'Joseph, son of David, do not fear to take Mary as your wife, for that which is conceived in her is of the Holy Spirit. She will bear a son, and you are to call his name Jesus, for he will save his people from their sins.' When Joseph awoke, he did as the angel had instructed him, and took me as his wife. However, we didn't know each other as husband and wife[9] until after the child was born."

"Since both of you lived in Nazareth, is that where Jesus was born?" Joshua asked.

"That's what we had planned, but the Romans had other ideas. Apparently, Caesar Augustus decided to levy a new tax on all the peoples across his great and mighty empire, but he first needed to

---

[8] Jewish betrothals usually lasted from one to fifteen months, with most being about a year long.

[9] i.e., they were not sexually intimate.

conduct a census so he would know approximately how many people there were and where they were located.

"The logical way would have been to conduct the census of the people where they lived. But is that what Caesar ordered? Of course not! Maybe that would have been too logical a course of action for our Roman rulers. In any event, Caesar came up with the inexplicable idea of requiring everyone to go back to their ancestral homes. Since both Joseph and I were of the house and lineage of King David, we were therefore required to travel all the way to Bethlehem—just as I was about to give birth! Although Joseph got a donkey for me to ride, it was still a horribly long and hard journey."

"Did you make it to Bethlehem safely?"

"Yes—but when we got to Bethlehem, we discovered there was no room for us. Not only was the inn filled beyond its capacity, but the local citizens had already taken in as many travelers as they could. Even our relatives who lived there had filled their guest room! Luckily, the innkeeper took pity on us—primarily because of my condition—and he allowed us to stay in a nearby cave he used as a stable for his animals."

"How did that work?"

"Better than I would have expected," Mary answered. "During the night, I gave birth to my miracle child. We didn't have a doctor or a midwife or anyone else to help poor Joseph; he had to do it all. Well, not the labor, of course; I did that. But God was with us, and there were no complications despite the rather difficult circumstances. While I was going through my labor pains, Joseph had placed the cleanest straw he could find in the manger used as a feed trough for the stable animals. When our baby boy was born, we wrapped him in some soft clothes we had with us, and placed him in the manger as a makeshift crib."

Mary got to her feet, walked to the table next to the wall, and picked up a small loaf of bread. She broke it, gave part of it to James, handed the middle portion to Joshua, and kept the remainder for herself.

"Later that night a group of shepherds appeared at the mouth of the cave and asked permission to enter. At first I was afraid, but they said they had been sent by angels, who informed them that the Christ child had just been born in Bethlehem. They said they were terrified by the sight of the heavenly host and the glory of God that filled the landscape around them, and decided they had better immediately do exactly what the angels had said! After they had gawked at the baby for a few minutes, they nervously made their exit, but I noticed that they were glorifying and praising God for revealing his miracle to them."

"What did you think about that?" Joshua asked.

"Personally, I was glad it had happened. Although Joseph could not have been sweeter and more understanding throughout the entire ordeal, I suspected that he may still have had some questions about how virgin a birth this was, even after his dream or vision of the angel. Having total strangers show up claiming that the angelic hosts of heaven had announced the birth of the Christ child probably helped dispel any lingering doubts."

"What happened next?"

"Eight days later, Jesus was circumcised, and a few weeks after that we took the child to the temple in Jerusalem so that he could be dedicated and I could be purified[10] after giving birth to my son.

There was an old man there at the temple who introduced himself as Simeon. He claimed that the Holy Spirit had revealed to him that he would see the promised Messiah before he died. He also said that the Spirit had led him to be in the temple that particular day. He blessed all three of us, and praised and glorified God for allowing him to see the Messiah. There was also an old lady named Anna who basically did the same thing."

"Did you continue to live there in Bethlehem, or did you go back to Nazareth?"

"We stayed in Bethlehem, but we obviously couldn't stay in the cave indefinitely. As soon as we could find a small house we could afford to rent, we did so. Since Joseph was skilled as a carpenter, he did various odd jobs around town to help us make ends meet. The innkeeper was especially good at sending business our way.

"One evening we were startled by a procession of camels bearing a group of grandly dressed men. Their clothes were as fine as those worn by kings, though they said they were wise men from the East. I had no idea what they meant by that, but both Joseph and I decided not to ask questions. Our experiences with royalty, nobility and other really wealthy people has tended to be more negative than positive, if you know what I mean.

"Anyway, they wanted to see the new King of the Jews. Joseph and I looked at each other questioningly, and then realized they meant Jesus, who was then a toddler. And then these great and mighty men—and their bodyguards and other attendants—all bowed down and worshiped our baby. They then presented expensive gifts of gold, frankincense, and myrrh."

"How had they found you?" Joshua asked.

---

[10] A Jewish ceremony to officially mark the end of the mother's being ceremonially unclean after giving birth.

"Some of them said they had noticed a bright new star that had appeared over a year earlier. They had consulted their records and charts and determined that this was probably a sign that the promised king, for whom the Jews had been looking, had finally been born. They followed the star until they got to the road leading from Jericho to Jerusalem, but then lost sight of it due to the rocky cliffs and clouds. Since the Jericho road led upward to Jerusalem, the Jewish capital, they naturally assumed that the new king had been born there.

"They therefore went to the palace and asked, 'Where is the king of the Jews?' They were directed to the chambers of Herod the Great. The wise men asked him, 'Where is the *new* king of the Jews?'"

"Wait a minute," Joshua interrupted. "Didn't Herod consider himself to be the one and only king of the Jews?"

"Yes, and he didn't like any competition for his throne—but he knew better than to tell the wise men that. Although Herod apparently suspected they were talking about the Messiah prophesized by the prophets, he didn't have a clue where the new king would be. Herod summoned the chief priests and scribes, and demanded that they tell him where the Messiah would be born. They informed Herod that Bethlehem was the place. Herod then quizzed the wise men about when the star had appeared and sent them off to find this new king, but instructed them to then come back and tell him so that he too could worship the child."

"Did the wise men return to Herod after finding you?"

"No. God apparently sent the wise men dreams that night warning them not to return to Herod. They decided to immediately return to their own country by a different route."

"What did you do?" Joshua asked.

"Joseph also had a dream in which an angel of the Lord told him, 'Rise, take the young child and his mother and flee to Egypt. Remain there until I tell you to return, for Herod will search for the child to destroy him.' As you can imagine, we fled that same night. We were able to use the precious gifts given us by the wise men to finance the trip and to sustain us while we were in Egypt."

"So you were able to escape Herod's purge?"

"Yes, thanks be to the Lord, but we were devastated to learn how Bethlehem's other baby boys were butchered by that cruel man's soldiers. Joseph later had another dream in which an angel informed him that Herod the Great was dead. But when we got to Judea, we were afraid to stop there, since Herod's son Archelaus reigned in his father's place. We therefore kept traveling until we had returned to Nazareth."

"Very interesting and enlightening," Joshua remarked. "Do you recall anything else that was unusual about Jesus when he was growing up?"

"Not really all that much, except perhaps that he didn't seem to get into trouble or refuse to mind us," Mary answered. "Of course, since he was our firstborn, we didn't think about that all that much until we had other children. Jesus did set a rather high standard for the others to match, and I fear that may have led to a certain amount of hard feelings and jealousy."

Joshua glanced over at James, who was ignoring them while diligently staining the wood. *A bit too diligently,* Joshua thought to himself.

"Jesus helped Joseph in the carpenter shop until my husband died a few years ago," Mary continued, "and he has served as the man of the house until he moved out a couple of months ago. Otherwise, I don't recall anything particularly remarkable."

"Wait a minute!" Mary corrected herself. "There was one thing you might be interested in. Each year we would make the long journey to Jerusalem for the Feast of the Passover. We would typically join a caravan of others who were also going. As is normally the custom, each of us would travel with friends or acquaintances also making the trip. Thus, Joseph would visit with other men during the day, while I remained with the women. The children would play with other children about their same age. Then we would gather back together again for the evening meal and prayer time before going to sleep.

"We followed the same schedule each year until the time when Jesus was twelve years old. That year when the days of the feast were ended, Jesus did not rejoin the caravan—but we didn't realize that he had stayed in Jerusalem until we couldn't find him after traveling for one complete day. After verifying that he was nowhere in the caravan and that none of our friends or relatives had seen him all day, we returned to Jerusalem and searched diligently for him for three days. We finally found him in the temple sitting among the teachers, listening to them and asking questions. All who heard him were amazed at his understanding of the scriptures and the answers he gave to the teachers' questions."

"What did you do?"

"I ran to him and asked him, 'Child, why have you treated us this way? Your father and I have been searching for you in sorrow and anguish, not knowing where you were or if you were even still alive.'

"Jesus appeared surprised at my words and asked me, 'Why did you need to search for me? Didn't you know that I must be in my Father's house and doing my Father's business?' Nevertheless, he came with us without further comment or delay, leaving behind some amazed teachers of the Law of Moses. But that's about the only thing I really remember at the moment as being particularly out of the ordinary."

Jesus in the Temple

After both investigators reported back to Joseph of Arimathea, he made arrangements with Nicodemus for a visit. Since it was almost time for the Jewish Passover, the two men decided that the most convenient arrangement would be for Joseph and his wife, Esther, to stay at Nicodemus' house throughout the Passover celebration rather than travel back to their home in Arimathea each night. This arrangement also allowed the two men to visit quietly regarding what Joseph's investigators had learned about Jesus.

When Joseph finished reading the notes his investigators had made on their wax tablets along with the notes he himself had made while talking with his men, he realized Nicodemus had a stunned look on his face.

"Is something wrong, Nicodemus?" he asked.

"This time it is you who have given me a great deal to think about, my friend. You and Esther are still planning on staying with us through Passover, aren't you?"

"If that is still agreeable with you."

"Oh, most definitely. That should give us both more time to track down leads and information, and then to compare notes each day."

"What do you have in mind?" Joseph asked.

"Do you have contacts around Bethlehem you can trust?

"I do."

"See if you can find any shepherds who can either confirm or refute the account of the angelic hosts appearing and announcing the birth of the Messiah in Bethlehem," said Nicodemus. "For that matter, if they were really as excited as Mary claims, they should have told other people. See what you can find out."

"All right," Joseph responded.

"I should be able to use my sources to either confirm or deny the stories about Zacharias and the wise men, though you may also have contacts that can help. Are there any records that wise men— probably from the area around ancient Babylon—were watching the heavens for some sign? For that matter, is there any record of their following a star to Judea?"

"I can send a message with a caravan that will be leaving tomorrow morning."

"I can personally confirm Mary's account about the young lad confounding the teachers at the temple," Nicodemus continued. "I was one of the teachers who were amazed at the boy's knowledge of scripture and grasp of its significance. As I recall, he asked exceedingly penetrating questions that cut through the ritualism, dogma, and traditions we have added to the original scripture. I had the uncomfortable feeling that this young boy knew the true meanings of God's commandments far better than I did. In fact, it was that unsettling experience that largely prompted my deeper probing of the scriptures—which in turn led to my being accepted as an expert on the law and the prophets."

"You had never mentioned that to me previously, Nicodemus."

"Well, Joseph, I can't say it is one of my prouder moments. How would you feel if a young boy upstaged you in your area of expertise?"

"I would probably also be hesitant to mention it to others," Joseph laughed.

"Mary's account indicates that she is related to John, and that she even stayed with John's parents for several months prior to his birth. That raises the specter of possible collusion or even conspiracy between John and Jesus. Of course, that could happen even if they were not related—but the relationship increases the odds."

"Even if blatant collusion were to exist, that does not mean that what John said about Jesus is necessarily false, does it?" Joseph asked.

"No, no—you are quite correct," Nicodemus responded. "Nevertheless, I must guard against letting my interest in the promised Messiah cause me to not be as objective and diligent as I should be. I noted an interesting dichotomy—possibly even a paradox—in Joshua's account of what Mary told him. On the one hand, the shepherds and the people at the temple referred to the child as being the promised Messiah or Christ. However, the angelic messages to both Mary and Joseph instructed them to name the boy Jesus because he would save his people from their sins. That is not necessarily the normal job description we Jews would give for the anticipated Messiah. We have been looking for a great military or political ruler who will reestablish the might and glory of Israel as his ancestor David had done—except that this time the kingdom would last forever. I need to mull about that quite a bit more and may need to reexamine scripture on that point. It is likely that those issues will need to wait until a later time, though."

Nicodemus' face broke into a broad grin. "Excuse me, Joseph," he said, "but the beautiful irony of what Mary said has just blossomed in my consciousness. Can you imagine what Annas, Caiaphas, Matthias and some of their clique would say if Jesus does indeed turn out to be the Messiah?"

"What do you mean?" asked Joseph.

"Well, do you remember how much stock they put on being well-educated, well-connected to the elite or powerful people of the land, and of the upper echelons of Judea—and how much they belittle the rustic folk from Galilee as being inferior to them? What would they say or do if the Messiah turned out to be born to unlettered country people from Nazareth—of all places—in Galilee? Plus, Jesus' legal father was a humble workman far removed from anything our priestly friends would consider even remotely appropriate for the family of the Messiah—and the new king's birth was announced to simple shepherds, but not to any of the religious leaders.

"However, the thing that especially impressed me was how God may have used almighty Augustus Caesar to get that humble rustic couple to Bethlehem in time for the birth to take place where God's prophet had said it would occur. As Mary told your investigator, nothing is impossible with God!

"Nevertheless, I am rather skeptical of her story. Does she really expect us to believe she was impregnated by God? I can't get over the feeling that she has seized upon this blasphemous tale to excuse an illegitimate child."

"I agree. It seems strange to me that the same God who forbids sexual relations outside of marriage would deliberately impregnate a virgin."

"Good point, Joseph. Somehow that sounds more like the gods of Greek and Roman mythology, doesn't it?"

"That it does. Do you think we should dismiss her account?" Joseph asked.

"No, but we should check it out as thoroughly as we can. Since I have access to the official temple records, I should be able to check those records regarding what you have told me, and could then meet with you in the synagogue of the temple's royal portico after we have finished the morning prayers."

"Agreed," Joseph replied.

*****

Nicodemus rose early the next day and spent the morning hours searching through old temple records. His efforts were rewarded when he found a notation that the priestly division of Abijah had been assigned duties in the temple at the time Mary's narrative indicated Zacharias was there.

Nicodemus then found a priest named Amasa who also was of the priestly division of Abijah and who had served in the temple with Zacharias.

"The priests cast lots to determine their duties," Amasa said, "and Zacharias was chosen to enter the Holy Place of the temple and tend to the burning of incense. He was in the Holy Place for an abnormally long time—and when he reappeared, he was unable to speak. Through hand signs and writings, Zacharias indicated that he had seen an angel, but had been made mute by the angel when he disbelieved the angel's words that his barren wife would bear him a son."

Excited by his findings, Nicodemus hurried to the appointed synagogue to meet with Joseph. He had only been there a few minutes when Joseph walked briskly up to his side and quietly said, "I met with Joshua early this morning and then sent him to Bethlehem to see if he can find anything that either confirms or refutes the story about the shepherds." Joseph then added, "I also sent a dispatch to my office in Seleucia of Mesopotamia asking that any records regarding the wise men be checked."

"Very good, Joseph," Nicodemus commented, and then told his friend about his visit with Amasa.

"It would appear, then, that Mary's story is corroborated on at least that point," Joseph observed.

"So it would seem, Joseph. So it would seem." As the two men had been talking, they had walked out of the synagogue and into the area where the Royal Portico opened into the Court of the Gentiles. Joseph suddenly made a waving motion to someone across the courtyard.

"Eh, what is it, Joseph? Who do you see?" Nicodemus asked.

"Excuse me a moment," Joseph replied. "I will return in a few minutes."

Joseph trotted across the Court of the Gentiles until he reached a man Nicodemus did not recognize. Then both men returned to Nicodemus.

"Nicodemus, old friend, I'd like you to meet Bartholomew," Joseph said. "Bartholomew is the agent I assigned to follow Jesus."

"Then why is he here at the temple?" Nicodemus asked.

"Because Jesus is now here at the temple," Bartholomew said, pointing to a group of men that stood on the opposite side of the courtyard near some of the money changers. "He's the tall brown-bearded man in light brown robes with a white head cloth. The men that are with him are his disciples."

Nicodemus turned to watch the man of whom he had heard so much. Although Jesus seemed to be quietly listening and observing the transactions being conducted by the money changers, it appeared to Nicodemus that something was causing Jesus to become increasingly upset. Jesus then moved over to the area where sheep, oxen, and doves were being sold to penitents who needed a proper sacrifice. Jesus watched as several families were turned back by the priests because the animals they had brought with them did not meet the priests' standards. The dejected people had no choice but to purchase livestock offered by the temple sellers, who took the rejected animals as trades toward the required purchase price. Nicodemus knew that such "rejects" would typically be sold a week or two later as prime sacrificial animals. The practice netted a hefty profit for the high priest's coffers.

Jesus, however, did not appear to be amused. Instead, he stalked over to an area where some loose cords were lying on the ground. He made a whip out of the cords and then turned on the livestock sellers with a vengeance. Brandishing the whip as a weapon, Jesus overturned their tables.

"Take these things out of here!" he ordered. "Do not make my Father's house a market place!" Jesus then also turned over the tables of the money changers.

Attracted by the commotion, Caiaphas hurried to where Jesus continued his assault on the tables. "Just what do you think you are doing?" the priest demanded.

"It is written," Jesus replied, "'my house shall be called a house of prayer'—but you have turned it into a den of thieves."

"I am high priest of this temple," Caiaphas responded haughtily, "and I have authorized these people to offer their services as a convenience to the people. What sign can you show us for your authority to overturn these tables and cause such a disruption?"

"Destroy this temple," Jesus said, "and in three days I will raise it up."

"You are a madman!" interjected Matthias, who stood beside Caiaphas. "This temple has taken forty-six years to build—and it is still being worked on. Yet you claim you will rebuild it in only three days!"

Nevertheless, Nicodemus noted with wonder that Jesus' presence was so commanding that he appeared to have a greater aura of authority than did the Jewish officials who opposed him. Neither Caiaphas nor Matthias could maintain eye contact with Jesus. Rather, Matthias soon hung his head toward the ground, while Caiaphas moved over to another group of Jewish leaders. Money changers frantically picked up spilled coins, and livestock sellers chased and rounded up their loose animals.

Jesus, on the other hand, turned to the crowd of people that had been attracted by the commotion and began teaching them as he sat down in an area at the top of the steps near the portico where Jewish rabbis often discussed points of Mosaic Law.

"Do not allow yourselves to be so attracted to riches or monetary gain that you lose sight of the more important treasures God has in mind for you," he said.

"Similarly, do not store up treasures for yourselves here on earth, where moths and rust destroy and where thieves break in and steal. Rather, store up for you and your family treasures in heaven. Remember that where your treasure is, there will your heart be also."

Crowds of people had been attracted by the commotion of tables being overturned and sacrificial animals running free. Now the crowds pressed in around Jesus as he continued his instruction.

"Just as a slave or a servant cannot properly serve two entirely different masters, neither can you serve both God and worldly desires. Remember that the first and greatest of all commandments is that you shall love the Lord your God with all your heart, with all your soul, with all your body, and with all that you are. If you put God and his kingdom first, then all these other things will be added to you."

"Who can properly concentrate on things of God when we don't have enough food to eat or when we don't have decent clothes to wear?" yelled a middle-aged man who did not appear to Nicodemus to be either poorly clothed or underfed.

"Stop being so concerned with worldly matters or needs of the flesh, such as what you are going to be eating or drinking, or about what clothes you plan to wear," Jesus replied. "Is not life more than food and the body more than clothing? Behold the birds of the air," he said while gesturing toward the heavens. "They neither sow nor reap, nor do they gather food into barns; yet your heavenly Father meets their needs and feeds them. Are you not of much greater value than those birds?" People in the crowd murmured their agreement.

"And why are you so anxious about your clothing?" Jesus continued. "Consider the lilies of the field and how they grow. They neither toil nor spin. Yet I say to you: Even Solomon in all his glory was not attired like one of these. If God is able to give such splendid attire to even the grasses of the field, which are here today and tomorrow are cast into the oven, will he not take care of you, oh you people of such little faith?"

Some of the listeners seemed uncomfortable at Jesus' words, but others were nudging each other and nodding approvingly.

"Would it be possible for me to meet privately with Jesus?" Nicodemus asked Bartholomew quietly.

"Probably. He's staying here in Jerusalem. When do you want to meet?"

"Tonight after the evening meal, if we could."

"Come with me, and I'll ask."

As Nicodemus, Bartholomew and Joseph made their way through the crowd toward Jesus and his disciples, Jesus concluded his remarks by saying, "Therefore, do not spend so much of your time worrying about what you shall eat, drink, or wear. Your heavenly

Father knows the things you need. I say again that you should seek first the kingdom of God and his righteousness, and all these other things will be added to you. Concern yourself rather with knowing your heavenly Father's plans for your life and then work to carry out those plans."

Jesus rose from the steps where he had been teaching and walked back to his disciples. Bartholomew moved forward and said, "Master, these two men would like to meet with you privately after tonight's evening meal."

Jesus looked intently at Nicodemus and Joseph, then smiled and mused, "So two Pharisees who are members of the Great Sanhedrin wish to talk privately with me tonight? Very well. That can be arranged."

Jesus turned to a disciple named John and said, "After we have finished the evening meal and prayers, meet these men at the Portico of Solomon and then lead them to me."

Night Meeting

"What did you think about Jesus?" Joseph asked Nicodemus as they reviewed the young rabbi's teachings while walking back toward Nicodemus' house.

"Whatever it was that I was expecting," Nicodemus replied, "Jesus definitely was not it."

"What do you mean?"

"I'm not sure, Joseph. I'm just not sure. I suppose I expected someone who was brasher, more impulsive, less practical, more provocative, and with less command of presence and authority."

"Oh, so are you telling me that someone who overturns the tables of the money changers, drives out the livestock sellers, and threatens folks in the temple with a whip is not brash, impulsive or provocative enough to meet your standards of decorum?"

"You know very well that that is not what I was referring to," Nicodemus said with faux petulance. "Although," he added as an afterthought, "it was most interesting to see how his presence dominated even Caiaphas and Matthias. They both backed down to Jesus, and neither acted as if he even thought about summoning the temple guards."

"I don't think I've ever seen anything like it," Joseph commented. "Well, not unless you count that time the Roman centurion marched into the temple to quell a small riot—but he had a hundred armed soldiers with him. Jesus stood alone. But go ahead and give me the reasons for your assessment."

"Jesus doesn't act like most teachers."

"What do you mean?" asked Joseph.

"Most teachers either expound on the subtleties of the Mosaic Law, or they quote scripture and give their interpretations of what the scripture might mean, or they cite some other authority. Jesus didn't do any of that."

"I thought that what Jesus said seemed to be based on scriptures," Joseph objected.

"Oh sure, what he said was scriptural—but it was not done as a scholarly thesis or reference," Nicodemus responded. "Rather, it was part of an internalized message that flowed naturally out of him. It was almost as if God himself was revealing the reasons for the law and the lessons that should be learned from it. Although his message was consistent with God's word, Jesus didn't really seem to need other authority; he *was* authority."

"That's putting it mildly!" Joseph quipped.

"Also, Jesus' rhetoric was not an inflammatory speech calculated to rouse the rabble against their Roman oppressors, as is typically the case with self-appointed Messiahs or pseudo-leaders of the people. Rather, his message was an intelligent discourse regarding greed and materialism, which may possibly have been teaching points connected with his cleansing of the temple a few minutes earlier."

"What are you hoping to learn from tonight's meeting with Jesus?"

"Several things: Does he himself make any claim to be the Christ? If so, then what type of kingdom is he attempting to establish? We have always assumed that it would be political or military in nature, but I have yet to hear him address such matters. Rather, he seems to be confining himself to spiritual issues and our relationships with

God and with other people. I have yet to see how that is really consistent with our expectations for the Messiah. Nevertheless, the central question for me is whether he actually is the Messiah."

*****

John led Nicodemus and Joseph along the narrow Jerusalem streets to a house in the Upper City not far from the temple. Although the house was nowhere nearly as grand as Nicodemus' home, it was still much more spacious than those of most of the people. As they entered, a servant washed their hands and feet. Jesus politely excused himself from a group of people with whom he had been visiting and joined John, Joseph and Nicodemus in a private chamber.

Four wooden chairs surrounded a small wooden table on which a bowl of grapes had been placed. Oil lamps along the walls of the room provided lighting. Jesus sat in one of the chairs and gestured to the other men to join him.

"Rabbi," Nicodemus said to Jesus, "we know that you are a teacher who has come from God, for no man can do these miracles that you are doing unless God is with him."

"I tell you truly," Jesus replied, "unless a man is born anew, he cannot see the kingdom of God."

"What!" Nicodemus exclaimed. "How can a man be born when he is old? Can he enter a second time into his mother's womb and be born again?"

"I tell you again most truly," Jesus answered, "unless a man is born of water and the Spirit, he cannot enter the kingdom of God. That which is born of the flesh is flesh, and that which is born of the Spirit is spirit. Do not marvel that I said to you, 'You must be born anew.'"

Jesus reached forward to the bowl on the table in front of him, broke off a small bunch of grapes, ate one, and then continued. "The wind blows where it will, and you hear the sound of it, but you do not know where it comes from or where it goes. So it is with everyone who is born of the Spirit."

"How can these things be?" asked Nicodemus.

"Do you presume to be the teacher of Israel and yet do not understand this? I tell you truly, we are speaking of something we know when we talk of the wind. Similarly, I am testifying of something I have seen when I talk of the Spirit, but you apparently do not accept my testimony. If I have told you of earthly things and you do not believe, how will you believe if I tell you of heavenly things?"

Nicodemus opened his mouth as if he wanted to say something, and then thought better of it.

Jesus glanced at Joseph and then at John as he ate more grapes. When none of the others made a comment, Jesus added, "No one has ascended into heaven but he who came down from heaven, the Son of Man."

Joseph made a startled gasping sound, but then attempted to cover it by quickly coughing and grabbing a few grapes for himself.

Jesus studied Joseph for a moment before returning his attention to Nicodemus. "As Moses lifted up the serpent in the wilderness, even so must the Son of Man be lifted, that whoever believes in him may not perish, but rather have eternal life."

"Who is this Son of Man of whom you speak, and how does belief in him gain eternal life?" Nicodemus asked.

"God loved the world so much that he gave his one and only Son, that whoever believes in him should not perish, but should instead have eternal life."

Nicodemus stifled a surprised cry at Jesus' words. Jesus paused momentarily as he looked searchingly into Nicodemus' eyes. Nicodemus silently marveled at how the young rabbi's wide-set dark brown eyes seemed to be able to penetrate into his innermost being. He felt almost as though his thoughts were being read and his beliefs were being analyzed. Nicodemus had initially recoiled at Jesus' words, but now he felt a soothing peace he couldn't explain.

Then Jesus' ready smile returned and he continued his explanation. "God did not send his Son into the world to condemn it, but rather that the people of the world through him might be saved. He who believes in the Son is not condemned, but he who does not believe stands condemned, because he has not put his trust in the name of the only begotten Son of God."

"But Rabbi," Nicodemus objected, "how can God have a Son if there is one—and only one—God?"

"The old covenant required that a lamb be sacrificed as a substitute for a person's sin. The promised new covenant is at hand, and it will sacrifice the perfect Lamb of God." Jesus paused and ate the rest of the grapes in his cluster.

"How does that answer my question?" asked Nicodemus.

"Since only God can live a sinless life, he used a part of himself to make the perfect Lamb of God to be sacrificed under the new covenant and to serve as the light of the world."

"To serve as the light? What do you mean?" asked Joseph.

"The Messiah's role is to light the way of redemption to God and to be the true light that gives light and purpose to every man. Indeed, light has come into the world, but men loved darkness rather than light, because their deeds were evil. For everyone who practices evil hates the light and refuses to come to it, lest his deeds should be exposed. But he who seeks to live the truth comes to the light, that it may be shown that his deeds have been done in the reverence of God."

Jesus rose to his feet and walked to one of the oil lamps. Gesturing toward the lamp, he said, "People put a lamp on a stand so that it gives light to everyone in the house. In the same way, let your light shine before men, that they may see your good deeds and praise your Father in heaven."

He beckoned Nicodemus to rise and took Nicodemus' hands in his own. "Think about the things I have told you tonight, Nicodemus. Search the scriptures; search your heart; search your soul. You are not far from finding the kingdom of God—provided your mind and intellect allow you to do so. Again, prayerfully meditate on what I have said to you."

Turning to Joseph of Arimathea, Jesus added, "And you may be even closer to the kingdom of God."

Jesus then put his hands on both men and prayed, "Father, guide these men and help them to know your truth and your way. May they remember the covenants you made with Abraham, and may they have the courage to do what they know to be right. Amen."

Discussion in the Library

Joseph and Nicodemus walked in silence for several minutes after leaving the house. Finally Joseph broke the stillness by observing, "I sense that your interview with Jesus did not necessarily go the way you had anticipated."

"That may be the understatement of the year, my friend," Nicodemus softly replied. "I had carefully rehearsed in my mind the queries I would make that would naturally lead Jesus into confirming or denying whether he was the Messiah. Indeed, I felt compelled to determine his thoughts and attitudes regarding that topic. I wanted to know who this Jesus really is.

"Any man who can turn water into wine and who can heal blind or lame people with just a word or a touch has remarkable power. The miracles he has performed show that God is apparently with him—but to what extent? I had everything mapped out in my mind, and then immediately lost it when Jesus moved past my opening comments and didn't answer me or my implied questions directly."

Nicodemus had paused at the top of some steps that led down to a plaza. He turned toward Joseph, wrung his hands twice, and then continued in a slightly more agitated tone, "Jesus virtually ignored my questions regarding being the Messiah. Instead, he seemed to look into my mind and he challenged me on what is keeping me from having a close fellowship with God or an intimate knowledge of the kingdom of God. I can't explain it, but I had the same feelings he first stirred in me when as a twelve-year-old boy he moved past our ritualism and zeroed in on the heart of the matter. Only now he is a full-grown man instead of a pre-adolescent child."

As the two men reached his house, Nicodemus asked Joseph to join him in his library to continue their discussion. "Would you mind taking notes as I attempt to reconstruct my conversation with Jesus? Since you were also present, you can help refresh my memory on key points in order to keep our notes as accurate as possible."

"I would be most pleased to do as you suggest," Joseph replied.

The servant who had let them in and washed their feet led them to the library and lit the oil lamps there. Joseph reached into a basket and took out several wax tablets and a stylus. Then he sat down at a table to take notes, but Nicodemus continued standing and pacing back and forth across the room as he attempted to reconstruct his thoughts and emotions.

"Instead of answering my opening remark, Jesus told me in no uncertain terms that unless a man is born anew, he cannot see the kingdom of God. But what could that cryptic comment possibly mean? Why is it that one cannot even see the kingdom of God unless he is born *again*?"

"The interpretation you seemed to make while talking with Jesus was that a man must have a second physical birth—to return to his mother's womb and be reborn," Joseph remarked.

"Yes," Nicodemus responded. "I can't believe I blurted out something so silly and so obviously wrong. A second physical birth would accomplish nothing. Really great way to start out an interview, wasn't it?"

"Don't be too hard on yourself. Aren't the words used by Jesus similar to what we sometimes say when a Gentile proselyte converts to Judaism?"

"Yes, but that also could not be what Jesus meant, since he was addressing me—a Jew and teacher of the Jews—and since he made the statement into a blanket assertion embracing all mankind."

"Are you suggesting that Jesus was talking about everyone rather than just Jews?"

"I think so. Jesus seemed to be saying that merely being descended from Abraham may not be enough to qualify us to see the kingdom of God—even if we are Jewish members of the covenant nation who have followed all the Jewish laws and rituals. If that is the case, then the new birth is most likely some type of a spiritual birth or regeneration that makes us into a new creature or creation."

"If that's the case, why did Jesus say you must be born both of water and the Spirit?" Joseph asked.

Nicodemus paused before answering. "I'm not sure, Joseph. I can think of several possibilities, but will probably need to prayerfully search the scriptures and my own heart before coming to a conclusion."

"If you'll tell me the possibilities you're currently considering, I could put those down in my notes," Joseph offered.

"Well, being born of the Spirit is probably the easy part, since that would indicate that one needs to have a spiritual rebirth so that God's Spirit can dwell in the person. But what is meant by the water part?"

Nicodemus looked at Joseph, but received no answer.

After a moment, he continued, "Water *could* refer to a person being physically born, since the breaking of the water is generally the first stage in the birth process. If that is the case, Jesus could be saying that being physically born as a descendant of Abraham is not enough; we must also be reborn from above spiritually."

Nicodemus walked over to a vase containing an assortment of lilies and stroked the petal of one of the flowers as he sorted out his thoughts. "Or water could possibly refer to baptism, since John was calling for people to repent and be baptized, and Jesus reportedly asked to be baptized in order to fulfill all the obligations of righteousness."

Nicodemus picked up a wax tablet and ran his forefinger across its surface before continuing, "Or water could possibly be referring to the cleansing power needed for one to become righteous before God, as Ezekiel's association between water and God's Spirit might suggest. There may be other possible meanings as well, but I'll have to consider them later."

Nicodemus waited for Joseph to finish writing his prior comments before concluding, "Whatever he means, Jesus emphasized that it is absolutely imperative that a person *must* be born again or *must* be born anew from above spiritually in order to see the kingdom of God. If Jesus is sent from God—as he claims and as I strongly suspect may be the case—then it is important that we search the scriptures and prayerfully consider what is truly required to obtain the spiritual rebirth Jesus talked about."

Nicodemus picked up a bowl of grapes and set it down on the table where Joseph was taking notes.

"I cannot tell you how much Jesus' words stung me when he asked me how I could presume to be Israel's spiritual teacher if I did not understand the spiritual things of which he spoke," Nicodemus said as he broke off a small bunch of grapes. "Nevertheless, he did say that we both are close to the kingdom of God. Although I am not certain I accept his analysis of our spiritual condition, I am also not sure I can reject it out of hand. I know that my own prayerful study of scriptures has not fully satisfied me. I don't have the calm assurance Jesus seems to have—but it is something I desire very much."

"Jesus also said something about coming down from heaven," Joseph pointed out. "Does that mean he is laying claim to being either God or the Son of God?"

"I think he is at least claiming that his origin is of heaven, which would be somewhat similar to what Mary claims the angel Gabriel told her would happen if she agreed to bear the Christ child," Nicodemus answered. "This is also a concept that I must really think and pray about. A week ago, I would have branded any claim that God could have a son as being blatant blasphemy. After what Mary told Joshua and Jesus told us tonight, I am not as sure. Let's re-examine his statements and claims while they are still fresh in our minds."

"I think that would be wise," Joseph agreed.

"Jesus called himself the Son of Man," Nicodemus pointed out. "Since he also later referred to himself as being the Son of God, I don't think Jesus was saying he is the son of an earthly father. Rather, I think he is laying claim to being the one of whom the prophet Daniel spoke when Daniel said that he had a vision of the Son of Man coming with the clouds of heaven."[11]

"Sorry," Joseph said, "but I don't remember that vision."

"Daniel said that in his vision, the Son of Man was led into the presence of the Ancient of Days—whom I assume is God Almighty—and was given authority, glory and sovereign power. Daniel said all peoples, nations, and men of every language worshiped him. The Son of Man's kingdom was said to be an everlasting dominion that will not pass away, and his kingdom is one that will never be

---

[11] Dan. 7:13-14.

destroyed. In other words, by referring to himself as the Son of Man, Jesus may be laying claim to being the Messiah we have been waiting for all these centuries."

"My goodness!" Joseph exclaimed. "That potential meaning had totally escaped me."

"It will probably escape almost everybody, but it may have been an indirect answer to my intended line of questioning. Unfortunately, I was still reeling from everything else Jesus was saying to me and failed to really follow up on it. In fact, I didn't fully grasp the significance myself until a few moments ago when we started reflecting on his words."

Nicodemus stopped his pacing and remained rooted to one spot for several long moments. As the silence became stifling, Joseph glanced up from writing on his wax tablet and asked, "Is anything wrong?"

"Wrong? No, I don't think so," Nicodemus answered. "I was just wondering to myself if there might be even more meaning to Jesus' calling himself the Son of Man."

"What do you mean?"

"The Son of Man appears in Daniel's vision along with four unusual beasts that represent four powerful empires. It just dawned on me that Daniel's description of the fourth beast—the beast with iron teeth—may be another representation of the Roman Empire. Do you remember our earlier discussion of Daniel's interpretation of King Nebuchadnezzar's dream?"

"You mean as we were walking back to Jerusalem after observing John the Baptist?"

Nicodemus nodded affirmatively.

"Yes, I remember," Joseph answered. "The statue represented the four great empires from Daniel's time to the time of the Messiah."

79

"Daniel's vision of the four beasts might be a similar representation," Nicodemus said. "If so, then Babylonia is symbolized by the lion with eagle's wings, the bear with three ribs in its mouth stands for the Medes and Persians, the Greeks under Alexander the Great are the leopard with four wings and four heads, and the fearsome beast with iron teeth represents Rome—and the Son of Man comes during the time of the fourth empire."

"What did Jesus mean by his reference to Moses' lifting up the serpent in the wilderness?" Joseph asked.

"After Moses had led the children of Israel out of Egypt, they traveled through the wilderness. When the people murmured and complained about the trials they were experiencing and claimed they would have been better off to have remained as slaves to the Egyptians, God sent snakes to discipline them. It worked. The people repented and begged God to forgive them. God instructed Moses to make a bronze image of a snake and to raise it up on a pole. If a person who had been bitten by a snake looked upon the bronze serpent, that person would be healed."

"I remember that much," Joseph said, "but what did Jesus mean by it?"

"Our rabbinical teaching regarding this point is that as the children of Israel lifted up their eyes, not merely to the bronze serpent but also to their God, they were able to receive God's mercy, forgiveness and redemption. Thus, they who would otherwise be dead because of the serpents' bites would now be given life anew by God's merciful provisions and redemptive powers."

"But Jesus said that the Son of Man must be lifted up in the same fashion so that whoever believes in him may not perish but have eternal life," Joseph protested. "What does *that* mean?"

"I don't know, Joseph. I just don't know. I think it must have something to do with his statement about God loving the world so much that he gave his one and only Son so that whoever believes in him should not perish, but will have eternal life—but how that works, I just don't know.

"There are, however, some things we can at least surmise from those statements. First, Jesus is obviously claiming to be the one and only Son of God. Again, this is a statement I would have regarded as being the worst kind of blasphemy prior to hearing Joshua's report. It may still be blasphemy, but I want to investigate this whole matter more closely before jumping to that conclusion."

Joseph nodded and said, "I agree."

"Second," Nicodemus continued, "Jesus talked about how much God loves the entire world. I have been looking for a Jewish Messiah who would establish an everlasting Jewish kingdom. That does not appear to be what Jesus is saying. Again, I must search the scriptures more thoroughly on this point.

"Third, Jesus seems to be saying that we can only have everlasting life if we believe in him. What does that mean?"

"I don't know," Joseph confessed.

"He compounds that statement by stating the reverse; anyone who does not so believe is condemned. In other words, there seems to be some connection between believing in Jesus and the new birth he had mentioned earlier. Both those comments may also be tied into what the angel Gabriel allegedly told Jesus' parents: Jesus would save his people from their sins."

When Nicodemus remained silent for a few moments, Joseph looked up and asked, "What about those comments regarding the light of the world?"

81

"Jesus indicated that the Messiah's mission was to give light and purpose to people, and to light the way of redemption to God. He then said that the light he talked of has come into the world."

"Wouldn't that be an answer to your questions about whether he claims to be the Messiah?"

"You may be right," Nicodemus mused as he rolled a grape between his forefinger and thumb. "He may have answered my questions after all." He stood silently for a few moments, chuckled softly and then added, "Finally, there is also the matter of the words Jesus used when he prayed for us at the end of our meeting."

"What do you mean?" Joseph asked.

"Jesus laid his hands on us and prayed that the heavenly Father would guide us and help us to know God's truth and God's way. What truth and way was he referring to?"

Joseph merely shrugged and shook his head.

"He also prayed that we would remember God's covenant with Abraham, and that we might have the courage to do what we know to be right."

"Didn't God make several covenants with Abraham?"

"Yes. The first one was before God changed Abram's name to Abraham. When God first called Abram, God said that if Abram would leave his country, his people and his father's household, and go to the land God would show him, then God would make him into a great nation, God would bless him, and eventually all peoples on earth would be blessed through Abram. I have always thought that the last portion of that promise meant that the Messiah would be descended from Abram and that the Messiah would be God's means of blessing all the peoples of the earth."

"Sounds reasonable to me," Joseph remarked.

"God led Abram to the land of Canaan and promised him that Canaan would be given to Abram's descendants," Nicodemus continued. "God later changed Abram's name—which meant *exalted father*—to Abraham, meaning *father of many,* and told him that he would be the father of many nations, but that one of those nations—the one descended from his son Isaac—would be God's special covenant nation. It was through this nation that the Messiah would come, and God promised again that all nations on earth will be blessed."

"That part of the covenant is often overlooked," Joseph remarked. "At least, I know that I have been guilty of forgetting it in my desire to have the Messiah come, overthrow our enemies and oppressors, and establish his everlasting kingdom."

"You're not the only one, Joseph. In fact, I suspect that Jesus may have been reminding me that although the Messiah would be the culmination of God's covenant with Abraham and his descendants, the Messiah's blessings would extend beyond just us Jews. That is something I think I had forgotten. There may be many other things of which I have similarly lost sight of in my anticipation of a Messiah who would deliver his people from Roman oppression. I fear that our work and investigation have only just begun."

"Are you depressed or sorry that you have begun this quest?" Joseph asked.

"Not at all, my friend. This could be the most important quest either of us has ever attempted."

"I agree, Nicodemus. I agree."

Part Two

Feast of Tabernacles

Perhaps the most popular celebration among all the annual Jewish feasts and holidays was the Feast of Tabernacles, also sometimes called Succoth or the Feast of Booths. During this seven-day festival, each Jewish family would construct a small stucco or tent-like structure in their yard or upon some other property they had secured for the occasion. The family would then typically move out of their home into the structure for the week-long celebratory period.

The purpose for moving into the small structure was to commemorate and remember the wilderness wanderings of the children of Israel prior to their reaching the Promised Land. Because the event occurred after the harvests had been gathered, it also served as a time of thanksgiving to the Lord for his blessings and for enriching their lives with the fruit of the land.

Because the focal point for the celebrations was the temple in Jerusalem, long caravans of Jewish pilgrims would make their way to Jerusalem from Galilee and from other places around the world. On each of the seven days, the Jewish people came to the temple bearing fruit as an offering along with palm and willow branches that were used to form a roof over the altar.

Nicodemus and Joseph joined the throng of people following the *cohen*, a specially chosen temple priest, as he took a golden pitcher and led other priests and the throng in a processional down to the Pool of Siloam, which was located in the southeastern corner of Jerusalem. The water in the pool came from Gihon, the only natural spring in the immediate vicinity of Jerusalem and the city's principal source for water, through a tunnel constructed by King Hezekiah—one of the greatest engineering feats of ancient history. By walling off the spring and moving its water through the tunnel under the Ophel hill, past the primary walls of the city and into the Pool of Siloam, Jerusalem had a sufficient supply of fresh water to allow the city to withstand enemy sieges.

As they wound their way down the dusty streets of Jerusalem, most of the people held branches of myrtle and willow tied together with palm fronds in their right hands and citrons or lemons in their left hands. Those persons who did not carry the branches and fruit symbolic of harvest waved or clapped their hands instead. The priests, Levites and others in the procession all joined together in singing:

Praise the LORD.
O servants of the LORD, praise the name of the LORD.
Let the name of the LORD be praised, both now and forevermore.
From the rising of the sun to the place where it sets,
The name of the LORD is to be praised.

Some of the people danced as they sang, but even those who had trouble carrying a tune were in high spirits as they sang the words of the Hillel[12], accompanied by the sounds of flutes, trumpets, hand-held harps and other musical instruments.

---

[12] Psalms 113-118.

As the throng pressed downward through the Lower City that stretched out from Temple Mount to the Pool of Siloam, it passed numerous open-air shops where potters, bakers, metal workers and various other craftsmen normally would be working at their trades. On this day, however, many of these shops were closed so that their owners could participate in the festivities.

When the procession reached the Pool of Siloam, the priests and Levites proceeded down the steps to the pool, and the remaining people in the procession followed. Nicodemus and Joseph positioned themselves next to one of the white columns on the terrace that surrounded the pool of water. A choir of Levites clad in white linen robes spread out around the pool and sang, "With joy you will draw water from the wells of salvation," while the *cohen* filled the golden pitcher with water and then lifted it up for all to see.

The priests and Levites then passed back through the crowd and led the procession back up to the temple, entering that structure through the Water Gate and proceeding through the Court of the Gentiles. At its center was a second enclosed compound, posted with signs warning in Greek and Latin, "No foreigner is allowed within the balustrades and embankment about the sanctuary. Whoever is caught will be personally responsible for his ensuing death." In other words, only Jews were permitted to pass through the large gates into the Court of Women.

As the joyous Jewish procession passed through those gates, the people again recited in unison the words of the prophet Isaiah, "With joy you will draw water from the wells of salvation." They then ascended the flight of fifteen stairs on the western side of the Court of Women that led to the Nicanor Gate. The Jewish men passed through the magnificent bronze doors that had been donated by Nicanor, a rich Jew from Alexandria, into the Court of Israel. The doors were left open, however, so that the Jewish women could observe the ceremony.

A low balustrade separated the Court of Israel from the Court of Priests, which normally was only accessible to the priests and Levites. The Feast of Tabernacles, however, was one of the rare occasions when others were permitted to approach the great altar of sacrifice in the center of the Court of Priests. Adult Jewish males circled the altar seven times in a joyous procession.

The *cohen* then delivered the golden pitcher to the *cohen hagadol* or high priest, who poured the water out over the altar as an offering to God, and as an act symbolizing the nation's prayers for rain. The ceremony also signified the outpouring of the *Ruach HaKodesh*—the Spirit of the Most High—on God's chosen people. On the final day of the event, the people would repeat the processional seven times.

The people also celebrated with music and dancing at night, as four massive candelabra known as menorahs lit the temple area. Levites chanted psalms, accompanied by the music of flutes.

Although some of the wealthier people had sufficient land within their own fenced estates to erect temporary structures in a relatively private location, most of the people either erected booths on the flat roofs of their houses or joined the pilgrims in the large tent cities that sprang up in or around Jerusalem. This arrangement naturally facilitated intermingling among the people. While the children played with others of similar ages and the women compared notes on child rearing and domestic affairs, the men usually discussed matters of religion, politics, and social events. Such conversations almost inevitably turned to a discussion of the promised Messiah, with accompanying arguments about various self-appointed leaders who might claim to be the Anointed One.

This year—far more than any year in the past—those discussions centered around a certain young rabbi or teacher known as Jesus of Nazareth, who had been openly preaching around the Sea of Galilee for the preceding couple of years. It was reported by many that he had performed many remarkable miracles, though some in the crowd questioned the validity of such claims. Although the opinions of the people were largely divided between those who thought that Jesus was at least a good man (and very likely a prophet of God) and those who thought he was a deceiver who was leading the people astray, it was common for many of the more favorable opinions to be expressed rather guardedly and quietly, since it was apparent that many of the Jewish religious leaders and authorities did not approve of the young teacher from Galilee. The religious leaders asserted that Jesus did not properly observe either the laws of Moses or the commandments of God, since he had healed several people on the Sabbath when he was in Jerusalem previously.

About halfway through the week-long celebration, Jesus himself appeared in the temple and began to teach. Those who heard him marveled at his knowledge of the scriptures, especially since his detractors had been belittling him because he had no formal training in the scriptures from any of the established Jewish teachers or scholars.

"God commanded us to observe the Sabbath day and keep it holy," a young Pharisee named Saul called out to Jesus. "Yet you have violated the Sabbath by working on that day. You have healed lepers, have given sight to the blind, and have made the lame walk—all on the Sabbath. How do you justify your actions?"

91

"Let me ask you a question," Jesus responded. "Moses commanded that a boy be circumcised on the eighth day after birth. If that day is the Sabbath, you still will circumcise him on that day so that the Law of Moses might not be broken. Why then are you angry with me because I made a man's entire body well on the Sabbath?" When Saul made no reply, Jesus continued by saying, "Do not judge merely according to your prejudices or appearances, but rather be honest and fair in your judgments." Those crowding around murmured their approval of Jesus' words, while Saul quietly simmered with rage.

*****

"What do you think?" Nicodemus asked Joseph as they later discussed the exchange between Jesus and Saul. "Both of us are Pharisees and members of the Sanhedrin. We have lived by the law and for the law all our lives. Yet the one we both believe could possibly be the Messiah heals on the Sabbath and allows his disciples to pluck grain from the stalks and grapes from the vine on the Sabbath."

Joseph sat silently for a minute. Then he stood and walked to a window before turning and answering, "Personally, I think Jesus makes a valid point about the Sabbath being made for man rather than the other way around."

"But we are specifically commanded to honor the Sabbath, to keep it holy and not to work on that day."

"Which part of that commandment says it is wrong to help other people who need healing—or any other kind of assistance—on the Sabbath?"

"Well, none of it," admitted Nicodemus. "But the law is clear that we must not turn it into just another work day. As Pharisees and members of the Sanhedrin, people look to us to set the example."

"Yes, and what they see is a group of men so obsessed with keeping not only the letter of the law but also all the extra rules and regulations that we have imposed that they have wholly forgotten the reasons for God's laws and commandments in the first place. Sorry, Nicodemus, but I'm with Jesus on this one."

Nicodemus looked at his friend but didn't say anything. After a moment, Joseph's countenance softened as he smiled and said, "How many times have you yourself complained of the overly legalistic mindset of our fellow Pharisees?"

Nicodemus thought about what Joseph had said. Then he also smiled, nodded, and admitted, "Legalism can be a cruel taskmaster. When we concentrate totally on the rules and regulations of the Mosaic law, we tend to either become proud and arrogant because we adhere to the law better than others—or we become fearful that we have failed to do something the law requires of us."

Joseph chuckled, "That pretty well describes the life style of the typical Pharisee."

"Not just the Pharisees, Joseph. David pleaded in the psalms for God to restore the joy of his salvation."

"I think that's one of the major things that Jesus has that separates him from the rest of us."

"What do you mean, Joseph?"

"Jesus has a joy that radiates out from him that is infectious."

"He does, doesn't he? He also has a sense of purpose that I find intriguing—and a peace I simply cannot understand. Yes, Joseph, the more I think about it, the more I think I may have to agree with you about the limitations of our legalistic mindset."

*****

Many of the people who were in the temple began asking each other openly whether Jesus could be the Messiah for whom they had been waiting. "After all," they said, "could any other prospective Messiah do more miracles than what this man's already done?"

Someone in the crowd pointed out that if Jesus were really the Messiah, why would the Jewish religious leaders and authorities desire to kill him? That comment caused several others to respond that those leaders must not be trying too hard, since Jesus was standing in the midst of the temple teaching openly.

On the seventh and last day of the Feast, known as the *Hoshana Rabbah,* the people repeated the seven-fold processional, culminating with the words "With joy you will draw water from the wells of salvation" and "Oh Lord, save us; Oh Lord, grant us success." At that point Jesus stood and cried with a loud voice, "If any man thirsts, let him come to me and drink. He who trusts in me, as the scripture said, out of his inmost being shall flow rivers of living water."

When they heard these words, some of the people exclaimed, "This is truly the Prophet!" or "At last the Messiah has come." Others yelled back, "He can't be the Messiah. He comes from Galilee."

Caiaphas called a detachment of temple guards to him and commanded them to arrest Jesus for provoking a disturbance. However, when the guards got to Jesus, they stood transfixed, listened to his words for a while, and then returned to Caiaphas, who by this time had summoned the priests, Sadducees and Pharisees to the synagogue in the temple's Royal Portico.

"Why didn't you bring us Jesus of Nazareth?" Caiaphas asked the guards. "Didn't I command you to arrest him?"

"No man ever spoke like that man!" answered the officers.

"Have you also been led astray?" Matthias asked bitterly. "You should notice that only the uneducated rabble is attracted to Jesus.

Those simpletons have not been properly educated and do not know the law. Those people are accursed and are proceeding to their own doom. Have any of the authorities or any of the Sadducees or Pharisees believed in him? No, of course not. We know better."

"I issued a clear order to my own guards to arrest that man," Caiaphas muttered to himself, shaking his head, "and yet they failed to carry out even that simple directive!"

"Does our law judge a man without first giving him a hearing and finding out what he is doing?" Nicodemus asked.

"Are you also from Galilee?" Caiaphas snapped. "Search the scriptures for yourself. You will find that no prophet comes from Galilee!"

Blasphemy?

"I tell you, Joseph: It was all I could do to force myself to remain silent when Caiaphas made his comment at this afternoon's meeting," Nicodemus said later as he and Joseph met privately in Nicodemus' library. "I practically had to bite my tongue to keep from reminding him that Jonah came from Galilee, that Isaiah said the Messiah would have a Galilean ministry, and from telling him that not only had we already searched the scripture, but we had also already confirmed that Jesus was born in Bethlehem rather than in Galilee."

"Yes," Joseph agreed. "Finding those shepherds plus the other people who remembered those remarkable events definitely sealed that particular point. Although we were unable to find similar documentation regarding the wise men, we were able to verify enough of that story that I feel confident we now know why old King Herod ordered the execution of Bethlehem's baby boys."

"I agree, Joseph," Nicodemus concurred. "I agree. But I still do not understand how he could be the Messiah unless he reestablishes King David's throne and overcomes those who oppress us."

"Oh, is that all you lack now?" Joseph asked. "I thought you were still hung up on whether it was blasphemy for Jesus to claim to be the Son of God."

"Well, that's true. Until very recently, my major objection was the claimed relationship between Jesus and the Lord God Almighty. After all, the Shema[13] says 'The Lord our God is one God.' The scriptures tell us in no uncertain terms that there is one—and only one—God who made all else. How then could God have a son? Wouldn't that cause there to be two gods instead of one?"

Joseph shrugged his shoulders but did not say anything.

When it became obvious that Joseph would prefer to avoid answering the question, Nicodemus nodded his head and said, "I have been diligently searching the scriptures and have found two passages that have helped clear up that problem for me. The first one was when God spoke to Moses out of the burning bush. God said he was sending Moses back to Pharaoh to bring the children of Israel out of Egypt."

"Wasn't that what Moses had been praying for?"

"Well, yes and no," Nicodemus replied. "Yes, in that he had been praying that God would remember his promises to Abraham, Isaac and Jacob, and would deliver the children of Israel out of bondage in Egypt—but no, in that Moses was appalled that God would even consider using him as God's agent."

"Sounds typical," Joseph quipped as he shook his head. "People haven't changed all that much, have they?"

"I can relate to Moses' reluctance to face the ruler of the world's most powerful nation," Nicodemus answered. "I couldn't even stand up to Caiaphas earlier today. But God wouldn't take no for an answer, and Moses eventually ran out of excuses. Moses then said to God, 'Suppose I go to the Israelites and say to them, "The God of

---

[13] Deuteronomy 6:4; can also refer to Deuteronomy 6:4-9 and 11:13-21, and Numbers 15:37-41.

your fathers has sent me to you," and they ask me, "What is his name?" Then what shall I tell them?'

"God answered with the name Yahweh, which can mean either I AM WHO I AM or I AM WHO I CHOOSE TO BE. God then told Moses to tell the Israelites that I AM had sent Moses to them.[14] The more I think about the name God chose for himself, the more implications I can see in that name."

"For instance?" Joseph prompted.

"Well, perhaps the easiest and most obvious point is that God *is*. We humans may debate with each other all we want to about whether there is a God, but whatever we decide among ourselves does not affect the actual existence of God. He still exists and is ultimately in control even if we puny humans have decided otherwise. Secondly, I AM is the eternal present tense. God is yesterday, is today, and is forever. He is not limited by time or distance, because those are dimensions of the universe he created. Since the Creator is not limited by the dimensions of his creation, he is omnipotent[15], omniscient[16], omnipresent[17] and eternal[18]. In other words, we serve a God without limits except as he chooses to limit himself."

"How can God limit himself?" Joseph asked.

"There probably may be several ways, but the one that readily comes to mind is that when God makes a promise or a covenant, he limits himself to abide by his bargain."

"How does that relate to Jesus' claim of being the Son of God?"

---

[14] Ex. 3:14-15.
[15] All powerful.
[16] The all-knowing Supreme Intelligence.
[17] Present at all times in every part and time of his universe.
[18] Having no beginning and no end.

"Well, Joseph, Genesis teaches us that God is the eternal spirit who created everything, who brought light out of darkness, and who brought order out of chaos. Jesus said that God is spirit, and his worshipers must worship him in spirit and in truth. Now couple those concepts with God's statement that he is who he chooses to be, and with the angel Gabriel's statement to Mary that God's Holy Spirit would come upon her, and that God's awesome power would overshadow her. Because the Lord God Almighty would use a part of his own pure energy to impregnate Mary, the holy one who would then be born to her would be called the Son of God. If God used a part of his own eternal essence to impregnate Mary, that part would still be the same one eternal God—but it would exist in human form and with certain human limitations. Although I have worked that much out for myself, I still don't understand *why* God would choose to do it this way. Nevertheless, it would explain how the Messiah could reign forever. After all, God is eternal."

"Very interesting—but I don't see how that answers your earlier questions about whether Jesus' claims constituted blasphemy."

"Thanks for reminding me, Joseph. I said earlier that there were a couple of scriptures that helped me solve that problem. The other scripture was a prophesy by Isaiah, who wrote:

For to us a child is born,
To us a son is given,
And the government will be on his shoulders.
And he will be called
Wonderful Counselor, Mighty God,
Everlasting Father, Prince of Peace.
Of the increase of his government and peace
There will be no end.
He will reign on David's throne
And over his kingdom,

Establishing and upholding it
With justice and righteousness
From that time on and forever.
The zeal of the Lord God Almighty
Will accomplish this.[19]

"Isaiah—who is very likely the greatest prophet in our history—is telling us that the promised Messiah would be a wonder-working counselor; *pelé*—the Hebrew word Isaiah used—is the same word as was used in Exodus to describe the wonders and miracles God did while delivering his people from Egypt. Do you know of anyone who has performed more miracles and wonders than Jesus?"

"More wonders than Jesus?" Joseph echoed. "Is that even possible?"

"Isaiah also said he would be the Prince of Peace who would institute a government of peace which would have no end. I think that probably means that the government established by the Messiah will bring peace to the world."

"Makes sense to me," Joseph nodded.

"But think of the other two terms Isaiah used. He said the Messiah would be called both the Mighty God—*el gibbor*—and the Everlasting Father. Both of those terms are reserved for God alone. Why then would Isaiah speak so positively about the Messiah being called those things? Why wouldn't it be blasphemy? Answer me, Joseph."

"I don't know," Joseph admitted.

"Isaiah gave us the answer right there in his prophesy. He told us that *the zeal of the Lord God Almighty will accomplish it!*"

---

[19] Isa. 9:6-7.

Nicodemus answered triumphantly. "If it is God himself who does it, how can it be blasphemy?"

Lazarus

Approximately two miles east of Jerusalem along the southeastern slope of the Mount of Olives was the small village of Bethany. Indeed, the village was close enough to Jerusalem that it could be considered a suburb of the city. A man named Lazarus lived in Bethany with his two sisters, Mary and Martha. The three siblings had welcomed Jesus and his disciples into their home on numerous occasions, and they not only counted the young rabbi as a close personal friend, teacher and comrade, but had also accepted him as their Lord and master as well.

As a result, Jesus seldom traveled to or from Jerusalem without at least stopping by their home for a brief visit, and it was not unusual for him to stay there during his visits to Jerusalem. It was also not unusual for Jesus to use a grassy area under some large shade trees near their home as a place to teach the crowds of people that tended to flock to hear him.

However, there was one visit that Jesus made to Bethany that stood out from all the others. Lazarus had become extremely ill, and the doctors gave him no hope of living. Mary and Martha therefore sent a courier to find Jesus and to ask him to immediately come to Lazarus' aid, since they firmly believed that only immediate intervention by Jesus could save their brother's life.

The courier eventually found Jesus preaching and teaching in Galilee, and told him, "Lord, Lazarus, whom you love as a brother, is at the point of death unless you save him." Jesus, however, continued his ministry in Galilee for an additional two days before journeying to Bethany.

When Jesus arrived at Bethany, he was informed that not only had Lazarus died, but that he had been buried for four days. A large group of mourners and friends were attempting to comfort Mary and Martha. Rather than moving through the crowds, Jesus stayed on the outskirts of Bethany and sent a message to the sisters that he had arrived. Martha immediately went out to meet him, but Mary remained at home and continued receiving the mourners and well-wishers.

Martha followed the messenger to the place where Jesus waited. When she caught sight of him, Martha started to run toward Jesus, but then halted momentarily, bit her lip, and wavered indecisively before finally turning and walking resolutely to the man who had been her last hope.

"Lord, I wish you could have come sooner," Martha said, shaking her head sadly. "If you had been here, my brother would not have died. But I know that even now God will give you whatever you ask."

Jesus said to her, "Your brother will rise again."

"Yes, Lord," Martha replied, "I know he will rise again in the resurrection at the last day."

Jesus responded, "I am the resurrection and the life. He who believes in me will live, even though he dies; and whoever lives and believes in me will never die. Do you believe this?"

"Yes, Lord," Martha answered. "I believe that you are the Messiah, the Son of God who was to come into the world."

"Where is your sister?" Jesus asked.

Martha went back to the house and told Mary, "The teacher is here and is asking for you." Mary hurriedly got to her feet and went outside.

Younger, vivacious and more energetic than her sister, Mary ran to where Jesus was waiting, fell at his feet, and wailed, "Oh, Lord, if you had only been here, my brother would not have died."

Jesus knelt down, placed his hand on Mary's shoulder, and gently asked, "Where have you laid him?"

Mary looked at Jesus through her tears and answered, "Come and see."

She led him past a stone wall lined with date palms and along a path that led to the small cave where Lazarus had been placed. A large stone had been laid across the entrance. Mary shook her head and sobbed, "He's in there. Why couldn't you have come sooner?"

Seeing her anguish, Jesus also wept for a few moments as he gently embraced Mary. "Have courage—and faith," he quietly said to her. Then Jesus turned toward some men near the tomb and commanded them, "Take away the stone."

"But Lord," Mary objected, "by this time there will be a bad odor, for he has been dead and buried for four days, and will be decomposing."

Jesus answered, "Didn't I tell you that if you only believe, you will see the glory of God?" When the stone had been removed, Jesus lifted his eyes to heaven and said, "Father, I thank you that you have heard me. I know you always hear me, but I say this for the benefit of the people standing here that they may know that I am acting in your authority and that you have sent me." Jesus then called in a loud voice, "Lazarus, come out!"

The crowd gazed fearfully at the dark opening to the tomb, from which wafted the sickening odor of decay mixed with the sweeter smell of burial oils and spices. One man muttered, "This is insane. Everyone knows a dead person's spirit hovers about his body for no longer than three days. Only God Almighty himself could raise Lazarus now."

For several long moments nothing disturbed the darkness and silence of the tomb. Then a vague white shape stumbled through the entrance to the tomb. The shape roughly approximated that of a man swaddled in funeral wrappings so that he could only hop and make the smallest of steps.

"Take off the grave clothes and let him go," Jesus ordered. Those closest to Lazarus then rushed to the man who had been resurrected from the dead and unwrapped the long strips of linen that bound his body and his face.

The hundreds of people who had gathered around the tomb were astounded. Most believed they had witnessed a mighty miracle, especially since a majority of them had been present for Lazarus' funeral and burial. Some had even bathed the dead body and wrapped it in the long linen grave clothes that shrouded Lazarus, and had added the burial spices to help offset the odor of death and decay.

"Glory be to God!" shouted several of the witnesses.

"Glory be! This must be God!" interjected one person.

"God in human form? Is that even possible?"

"Anything is possible with God."

"Or maybe Jesus is the Son of God!"

"More than one God? That's blasphemous."

"Maybe he is the promised Messiah!"

"Yes," responded a growing number of the crowd. "Surely Jesus is the Messiah."

"Can he successfully lead us against Rome?"

"Of course he can if he is the Messiah. Anyone who can raise the dead back to life can lead an army that does not need to fear death. They would be invincible!"

As some members of the crowd worked themselves into a frenzy of anticipation, Jesus and his disciples quietly disappeared into the house with Mary, Martha and Lazarus. The crowd of witnesses gradually dispersed, but they continued to excitedly discuss what they had seen and what it could mean for themselves and their nation.

Storm Clouds Gather

A much different reaction occurred among the Jewish religious leaders. When the report of Lazarus' resurrection reached the chief priests and Pharisees, they called an emergency meeting of the Sanhedrin, which served as both the governing and ruling council of the Jews and as the Jewish Supreme Court. Its seventy-one members were composed of Pharisees, Sadducees, scribes, elders, religious lawyers and other teachers of the law, and it was presided over by the high priest. In order to pass the laws of the nation, a minimum quorum of twenty-three members was required.

Although the office of high priest was hereditary and was supposed to be for life, that was changed by the Romans when they conquered Palestine. In effect, the office became a political appointment by the Roman government. They still allowed the position to be filled by a man meeting the hereditary requirements of Jewish law, but they also required him to be someone who would cooperate with the Romans.[20]

Three members of the Sanhedrin gave a full report of the resurrection and confirmed that they had personally interviewed the people who had washed and prepared the body for burial. Two of them had also been present for the funeral and had watched Lazarus

---

[20] Although the Romans allowed a high priest to serve only so long as he pleased them, the men who had previously served as the High Priest continued to be highly honored by the people, who still referred to them as being high priests or chief priests.

be placed into the tomb and the stone rolled across the door. They concluded by asserting, "Lazarus was definitely dead, and he definitely is now alive again."

"I thought four days was too long a time for one to be brought back to life again," remarked a scribe named David.

"That tradition is apparently incorrect," responded a legal scholar named Gamaliel.

"What are we accomplishing?" a Pharisee named Saul asked. "Here is this man performing many miraculous signs. If we let him go on like this, everyone will believe in him, and then the Romans will come and take away both our place and our nation."

"We can't allow that to happen," Matthias responded. "Our religion and laws are the binding force that holds our nation together. Why should some self-appointed Messiah be allowed to belittle the importance of observing the Sabbath or to continue attacking our authority? Now that he has also resurrected a man who was dead for four days, he may gain too great a following."

"This is true," said one of the three witnesses who had originally made their report to the Sanhedrin. "Many in the crowd of witnesses are ready to proclaim Jesus as the Messiah. They are already talking about how his army would not fear dying and would be unstoppable."

"That's madness," remarked Matthias. "Raising an isolated man is one thing. Going against the legions of Rome would invite annihilation. Our nation would be destroyed, and we would lose our positions of power."

"The real question is whether this was really a miracle," Simon said. "Isn't it obvious that all of this is merely an elaborate trick devised by Jesus and his close friend? Lazarus was only pretending to be dead. Both he and Jesus must die."

"You want to kill Lazarus again?" David joked, but his laughter quickly ceased when several members of the council silently glared at him.

"Or this might be through the power of Satan!" Simeon exclaimed. "If Jesus has any real power over death or the forces of darkness, it must be because he is in league with the Prince of Darkness himself!"

"You know nothing at all!" exclaimed Caiaphas. "It makes no real difference to us whether this alleged miracle is real or merely a deception or delusion. We cannot allow Jesus to attract enough of a following to incite the Romans to react. The Romans might blame us and even remove us from our positions of power. Think what that would do to our nation. Don't you realize that it is better for one man to die for the people than for the whole nation to perish? We must find a way to make it happen. Our task then, is to find a way to get rid of Jesus once and for all time. He must be found guilty of a crime punishable by death!"

Palm Sunday

Six days before the Passover, Jesus returned to Bethany. Mary, Martha and Lazarus attended a supper for him and his disciples at the house of a man known as Simon the leper, who had been previously healed by Jesus, and they all gave thanks that Lazarus was living and well again. Lazarus reclined at the table with Jesus while Martha served the food. Mary, however, took a litra[21] of very expensive spikenard perfume and anointed Jesus' feet. As she wiped his feet with her hair, the entire house was filled with the fragrance of the perfume.

Judas Iscariot, Jesus' disciple who served as treasurer for the group, complained at Mary's extravagance. "Why wasn't this perfume sold for three hundred denarii and the money given to the poor? That one bottle of perfume is worth a whole year's wages!"

Jesus replied, "Leave her alone. Let her do this in preparation for my burial. For you will have the poor with you always, but you will have me with you for only a short while longer."

When the Jewish people learned that Jesus was there, they came to Bethany in great numbers—both to listen to his teachings and to see Lazarus, who was now famous for having been raised from the

---

[21] About a pint or half liter.

dead. The chief priests discussed the growing acclaim Jesus and Lazarus were receiving and agreed among themselves that both men needed to be put to death.

On Sunday, Jesus left Bethany for Jerusalem and the Passover celebration. Jews from all over the world would gather for the celebration, and the numbers in Jerusalem would swell to over two million people. Over a quarter of a million lambs would typically be slain as the Jewish people remembered how God delivered the children of Israel from bondage in Egypt so many centuries earlier.

As they approached the village of Bethphage, Jesus sent forth two of his disciples, saying, "Go into the village just ahead, and as soon as you enter it you will find a donkey tied there, with her colt by her. Untie them and bring them to me. If anyone says anything to you, tell him that the Lord needs them, and he will send them at once."

The disciples did as instructed. While they were untying the animals, two men saw them and came running. One of them yelled, "What do you think you're doing? Why are you untying our donkeys?"

The disciples replied, "The Lord needs them."

"It's all right," the second owner said. "I recognize these men. They are disciples of Jesus, the rabbi who raised Lazarus from the dead."

"Very well," responded the first owner. "Take them with our blessings."

The disciples took the donkeys to Jesus. They spread their cloaks on the animals, and Jesus sat down on the colt. A great crowd of pilgrims joined them while others cut branches from the trees and spread them on the road. Then the crowd surrounded Jesus, some proceeding in front of him while others followed behind. The crowds of people shouted, "Hosanna to the Son of David! Blessed is he who comes in the name of the Lord! The Lord is God, and he has made his light shine upon us. With boughs in hand, join in the festal procession. Give thanks to the Lord, for he is good; his love endures forever. Hosanna in the highest!"

Hearing the tumult, those inside the city asked, "Who is this who is entering the city?"

The crowds replied, "This is the prophet Jesus, from Nazareth of Galilee." Excitement was high, since the word had spread about how Jesus had raised Lazarus even though he had been dead for four full days. Many were proclaiming Jesus as being the promised Messiah—and even those who were skeptical were still interested in seeing him and possibly witnessing another miracle.

As he watched Jesus riding into the city on a donkey, Nicodemus turned to Joseph and said, "It appears that Jesus may be staking his claim to being the Messiah."

"Oh?" asked Joseph. "Why do you say that?"

"He is riding into Jerusalem on a donkey."

"Wouldn't a horse or chariot be more suitable for a king such as the Messiah?"

"Not really, Joseph. Remember Zechariah's prophesy:

Rejoice greatly, O Daughter of Zion!
Shout, Daughter of Jerusalem!
See, your king comes to you,
Righteous and having salvation,
Gentle and riding on a donkey,
On a colt, the foal of a donkey.
I will take away the chariots from Ephraim
And the war-horses from Jerusalem,
And the battle bow will be broken.
He will proclaim peace to the nations.

His rule will extend from sea to sea
And from the River to the ends of the earth.[22]

"I would say that this triumphant entry into Jerusalem fulfills that prophesy, and the people certainly seem ready to proclaim him king. Let's see what he does this week."

*****

Each day during the Passover week, Jesus would follow the road from Bethany over the Mount of Olives and across the narrow Kidron Valley, pass through the tawny-colored sandstone walls of Jerusalem through the eastern gate, and then go to the temple, generally through the Beautiful Gate. Once again he cleansed the temple by overturning the tables of the money changers and the benches of those who sold doves and other livestock. Jesus also healed the blind and the lame, and taught those who gathered around him.

The chief priests and elders of the people came to him as he was teaching and asked him, "By what authority are you doing these things, and who gave you that authority?"

"I will also ask you one question," replied Jesus, "and if you answer me, then I will tell you by what authority I do these things. John's baptism—was it from heaven, or merely of human origin?"

The Jewish religious leaders then counseled among themselves, saying, "If we say, 'From heaven,' he will say to us, 'Then why did you not believe him?' But if we say, 'It was merely of human origin,' we will be in trouble with the people, for they all regard John as a prophet." So they answered Jesus, "We do not know and cannot tell."

---

[22] Zech. 9:9-10.

"Then I will not tell you by what authority I do these things," replied Jesus. "But what do you think about this? A man had two sons, and he went to the first one and said, 'Son, go work in the vineyard today.' And the son answered, 'I will, sir,' but he failed to go. The father went to the second son and said the same thing, and the son answered, 'I will not.' But afterward, he repented and went to the vineyard and worked as requested. Which of the two sons did the will of the father?"

"The second one," they replied.

"I tell you truly," said Jesus, "the tax collectors and harlots will enter the kingdom of God ahead of you. For John came to you preaching righteousness, and you did not believe him—but the tax collectors and harlots did. Because they repented of their sins and sought God's mercy, they were forgiven. But even after seeing that, you did not repent and believe him."

As Jesus was teaching, some of the scribes and Pharisees brought in a woman who had been caught in an adulterous affair and, placing her directly before Jesus, said to him, "Master, this woman was caught in the very act of adultery. Now Moses commanded us in the law that such a person should be stoned until dead. But what do you say?"

Jesus bent down and smoothed the dust into an even surface with his left palm. He then began to write on the ground with his right index finger.

"You heard the question, rabbi," one of the priests prompted. "What do you say?"

Unperturbed, Jesus continued writing in the dust.

"Don't you know what the Law of Moses says should be done with this woman?" a Pharisee named Saul chided.

"Actually, the Torah says we should stone both the woman and the man who committed adultery with her," a scribe named David answered.

"We all know what the Torah says," Saul snapped. "We want the rabbi to explain his position on it."

David nodded his head, suddenly realizing that the entire charade was an attempt to trap the young rabbi. They all knew that he had been preaching forgiveness, mercy and reconciliation. But if he now suggested anything other than the stoning required by Mosaic Law, they could denounce him as being a false teacher and a lawbreaker.

When the scribes and Pharisees asked him for his answer again, Jesus stood up and said to them, "Let the man among you who has never sinned cast the first stone." Then Jesus again bent down and continued writing on the ground.

David moved closer so that he could read what had been written in the dust. The Ten Commandments and several other laws of Moses had been outlined and had then been marked through with names of people who were apparently present at the gathering. He was startled to see the name "David" across part of the commandment not to covet. *Could that be me? Surely not. No one knew how much I wanted Joanna and how jealous I was of Simon when he married her. But word could have leaked about how badly I wanted to be named chief scribe. Could someone have told this Galilean teacher? No, that is probably some other David. But still … .* Knowing that he was not without sin, David dropped the stone he was holding and silently left the assembly.

One by one, others did the same. Being convicted by their own consciences, the woman's accusers melted away into the crowd, leaving her alone with Jesus.

Then Jesus stood and, seeing no one but the woman, said to her, "Woman, where are your accusers? Has no one condemned you?"

"No one, Lord," she answered.

"Neither do I condemn you," said Jesus as he used his foot to wipe out the litany of laws and sinners in the sand. "Go your way, and sin no more."

Although their previous attempts had been unsuccessful, the Pharisees were still determined to trap Jesus in his talk and teachings. After discussing the matter among themselves, several of them came to him. Their spokesman said, "Master, we know that you are honest and that you teach the way of God in truth, regardless of any man, for you are not influenced by the opinions and positions of men. Tell us therefore what you think. Is it lawful to pay taxes to Caesar, or not?"

Jesus glanced to his right, where a group of Roman soldiers was standing and observing the questioning by the religious authorities.[23] Jesus looked back at the Pharisees and answered, "Why do you test me, you hypocrites! Show me a tax coin." One of them handed him a denarius. "Whose likeness and inscription are these?" asked Jesus.

"Caesar's," they replied.

"Then give to Caesar the things that are Caesar's, and give to God the things that are God's," Jesus answered.

---

[23] It was the custom of the Roman governor to increase the number of Roman soldiers in and around Jerusalem during the Passover celebrations. The Roman garrison in the Fortress of Antonia that stood adjacent to and overlooking the temple would typically number up to six hundred men during the Passover. The Antonia stood on a precipice seventy-five feet high at the temple's northwest corner so that its battlements towered over the temple, and it was connected by two stairs that led to the Court of the Gentiles, and by an underground passage to the Court of Israel.

Later some of the Sadducees, a sect that believed and taught that there is no resurrection or spiritual life after a person's physical body dies,[24] posed the following question to Jesus: "Master, Moses said, 'If a man dies, leaving no children, his brother shall marry his widow and raise up children for his brother.' Now there were seven brothers among us. The first married and died, and having no children, left his wife to his brother. And so did the second, and the third, and all of them, including the seventh. Last of all, the woman died. Now in the resurrection, whose wife of the seven will she be? For all of them had her."

"You are in error," replied Jesus, "for you are ignorant of both the scriptures and the power of God. In the resurrection, people neither marry nor are given in marriage, but are like the angels in heaven. And concerning the resurrection of the dead, have you not read what was spoken to you by God himself when he spoke to Moses out of the burning bush?[25] 'I *am* the God of Abraham, the God of Isaac, and the God of Jacob.' He is not the God of the dead, but of the living."

One of the teachers of the law then asked Jesus, "Master, which is the greatest commandment in the law?"

Jesus immediately answered, "You shall love the Lord your God with all your heart, with all your soul, and with all your mind. This is

---

[24] The Sadducees only considered the Pentateuch—Genesis through Deuteronomy—as scripture. Since none of those books mention a resurrection of the dead, Sadducees did not believe in a resurrection or life after death. However, they had used this question previously to stump the Pharisees, who did believe in heavenly life after death.

[25] Although the Sadducees asked a question predicated upon a premise they themselves did not believe, Jesus did not mock them or ignore their query. Rather, he answered it directly—and then went on to address the underlying issue. Since the Sadducees only accepted the five "books of Moses" as acceptable authority, Jesus used that source as authority for his answer.

the greatest and most important commandment—and there is a second one like it: You shall love your neighbor as yourself. The whole of the law and the prophets rests on these two commandments."

While the Pharisees were assembled and were attempting to think of some other question that might successfully trap Jesus, he turned to them and asked, "What do you think about the Messiah? Whose son is he?"

"The son of David," they replied.

"Then how is it," asked Jesus, "that David, moved by the Spirit of God, calls him Lord, saying, 'The Lord said to my Lord, "Sit at my right hand until I put your enemies under your feet."' If David calls him Lord, how can he be his son?"[26]

From that time on, the religious leaders did not dare to ask Jesus any more questions in an effort to trap him.

*****

Jesus called his disciples to gather near him and he said to them, "You know that after two days the Passover will come. At that time the Son of Man will be delivered up to be crucified."

"Surely not, Master," said Simon the Zealot. "You are the Messiah. You must defeat the Romans and restore Israel to its glory."

"Simon," Jesus gently smiled. "I do not live to kill others to save a culture or a nation. Rather, I die to save the world."

---

[26] The Pharisees knew that both God's covenant with David and various prophesies said the Messiah would be a descendant of David. However, they were expecting a fully human Messiah who would deliver the Jewish people from their foreign oppressors. Jesus quoted Psalm 110:1 to show that David himself referred to the Messiah as being his divine Lord.

"How can you even talk of dying or of others taking your life?" asked John.

"John, John," Jesus said, shaking his head. "No one *takes* my life from me. Rather, I am voluntarily laying down my life of my own accord. This is the mission I have received from my Father. It is why I came into the world."

*****

The chief priests and the elders of the people gathered together in the palace of Caiaphas, the high priest, and discussed how they might arrest Jesus and then kill him. They agreed that they could not do it while he was publicly teaching in the temple or during the Feast, since such an action might provoke an uprising among the people. "We must find a time to arrest him when he is away from the crowds and relatively alone," they said.

Their opportunity seemed to present itself when Judas Iscariot, one of Jesus' inner circle of twelve disciples, went to the chief priests and asked, "What will you give me if I deliver him into your hands?" They answered by weighing out thirty pieces of silver for Judas. Thus the authorities took money from the temple treasury typically used to purchase sacrifices, and used it to purchase the supreme sacrifice—for thirty pieces of silver, the traditional legal price of a slave. From that time on, Judas watched for an opportunity to betray Jesus into their hands.

Passover and Lord's Supper

On the first day of Unleavened Bread, when the Passover lambs were being sacrificed in the temple, Jesus' disciples asked him, "Where do you want us to go to prepare for our eating of the Passover meal?"

Jesus turned to Peter and John and said, "Go into the city, and a man carrying a pitcher of water will meet you. Follow him, and wherever he enters, say to the master of the house, 'The Master says, "Where is the guest chamber where I will eat the Passover with my disciples?"' He will show you a large upper room, furnished and ready, and there you are to make preparations for us."

The disciples did as Jesus had directed, finding everything to be just as Jesus had said, and in that upper room they prepared the Passover. Not only did they purchase the food, drink, herbs and spices required for the Passover meal, but they also diligently searched the room to find and remove anything that might contain yeast—even tiny crumbs of bread.[27] When it was evening, Jesus arrived with the rest of the disciples.

Unfortunately, the disciples had been arguing among themselves as to which of them should be considered the most important.

---

[27] Because the Passover commemorates the Jews' deliverance from bondage in Egypt after the LORD passed over the Hebrew homes to strike down the Egyptians' firstborn, Jews begin the Passover with their Feast of Unleavened Bread, also known as the Passover Seder, in which they eat unleavened bread to help them remember the first Passover, when there was no time for the bread to rise.

Instead of preparing themselves for Passover by getting themselves into the proper frame of mind and by finding and removing any sin that would interfere with either their relationship with God or with their observance of Passover, they had been bickering as to which would be greatest in the Lord's kingdom. They therefore arrived at the upper room in a bad temper.

Due to their quarreling and because there were no servants present, none of them bothered to go through the typical Jewish custom of ceremonially washing their feet, even though their feet were covered with dirt from the dusty roads over which they had trudged. Instead, they stalked past the earthenware pitcher of water at the door and took their places around the table—still cross and in an argumentative frame of mind.

Jesus said to them, "The kings of the Gentiles lord it over their subjects, and those rulers are called *benefactors.* But it should not be that way among you. Instead, let the greatest among you act as if he were the least important, and let the one who leads desire to serve the others. Who is the greater, the one who sits at the table, or the one who waits the table and serves the food? Is it not the one who sits at the table? And yet I am among you as one who serves."

Then Jesus rose from the supper table, laid aside his outer garments, and took a towel and tied it around his waist. He poured water into a basin and began to wash the disciples' feet and to wipe them with the towel at his waist.[28]

When he had finished washing their feet, Jesus put his outer garments back on and sat down. He then asked his disciples, "Do you understand the meaning of what I have done to you and for you? You call me Master and Lord, and you are right, for that is what I am.

28Washing the feet of guests was typically the duty of slaves or the lowest-ranking servant available.

If I therefore—your Lord and Master—washed your feet, you ought also to wash one another's feet. In other words, look for ways you may serve and help one another. I have given you an example. Follow my example and do for others as I have done for you. I tell you truly, a servant is not greater than his master, nor is one who is sent greater than the one who sent him. If you know these things, you are blessed if you do them."

The Passover Seder began with the lighting of the two festival candles and the recitation of three blessings. First was a blessing of the kosher wine that was typically either unfermented grape juice or a mixture of wine and water. Four cups would normally be poured prior to commencement of the Seder, which corresponded with the four promises of God that would be observed later. Next came a blessing over the festival of Passover, which was followed by the *shehecheyanu* blessing that praised God for enabling the Jewish people to reach the current day.

"With great longing have I desired to eat this Passover with you before I suffer, for I tell you, I shall not eat it again until it is fulfilled in the kingdom of God," Jesus said as he dipped some of the *karpas*[29] and *marror*[30] into vinegar. He said a blessing, ate one, and then handed the others to each of his disciples. Next, Jesus broke the sweet unleavened bread known as *matzah* in half, placed one half aside for later use, and raised the other half up before his disciples and said, "This is the bread of misery which our fathers ate in the land of Egypt. All that are hungry, come and eat. All that are needy, come, keep the Pascha.[31]"

---

[29] Green vegetables.
[30] Bitter herbs.
[31] Transliteration of פֶּסַח, the Hebrew term for Passover.

Next came the reciting of the Passover story and a time of prayer, recitation of the Hallel Psalms,[32] and drinking from the cups of Passover wine that symbolized the four promises the Lord made to his people in Exodus: the cup of sanctification,[33] the cup of deliverance,[34] the cup of redemption,[35] and the cup of praise.[36] All the disciples joined Jesus in drinking from the first, second, and fourth cups. However, the third cup—the cup of redemption—was covered with a cloth and set symbolically aside for the prophet Elijah.

The disciples visited among themselves about various topics as they ate the Paschal meal. Jesus, however, appeared to be sorrowfully lost in thought before looking at his companions and saying, "I tell you truly, one of you will betray me." The disciples became agitated and sorrowful. One after another, they asked Jesus, "Is it I, Lord?"

"One who has dipped his hand in the dish with me will betray me," answered Jesus. "The Son of Man will go, of course, as it was written of him, but woe to that man by whom the Son of Man is betrayed! It would have been better for that man if he had not been born."

John asked, "Lord, who is it?"

"It is the one to whom I give this sop after I dip it," replied Jesus. When he had dipped the sop that consisted of the Paschal Lamb's flesh, a piece of unleavened bread, and bitter herbs, Jesus handed it

---

[32] Psalms 111-118.
[33] "I will bring you out from under the burdens of the Egyptians."
[34] "I will rescue you from their bondage."
[35] "I will redeem you with an outstretched arm."
[36] "I will take you as my people."

to Judas Iscariot and told him, "What you are going to do, do quickly."

Judas got up, took the sop with him, and immediately went out into the night.

Jesus then took the half loaf of bread that had earlier been set aside, blessed it, and broke it into pieces, which he gave to the remaining disciples. "Take this and eat it," he said, "for this is my body broken for you."

The disciples looked at each other questioningly, since they were not sure what Jesus meant by his words. Seeing their expressions, Jesus smiled and said, "You will have times in the future when you may wish to use the elements of this meal to help you remember what I am about to do for you. As often as you eat the unleavened bread, remember that I give my body as a sacrifice for your sins."

He then took the third cup—the cup of redemption often called "Elijah's cup" because it is normally left untouched and is reserved for the Prophet Elijah—and when he had given thanks, he gave it to them saying, "All of you drink of it. This is my blood of the new covenant, which is shed for many for the forgiveness of sins. I say to you, I will not drink again of the fruit of the vine until that day when I drink it anew with you in my Father's kingdom."

"But Master," said Peter. "Should we partake of Elijah's cup?"

"Elijah's cup represents the future redemption of all that shall occur when the Messiah ushers in the new covenant for all who believe in him. I am the Messiah and am now ushering in the new covenant. If you believe in me, then you should partake of the cup."

The words Jesus spoke gave evidence of his own belief as to what was the most central part of his ministry. He did not ask that his miracles be remembered or that his birth be commemorated. The memorial service that became known as the Lord's Supper[37] would instead remember his death and the price of redemption he paid.

After they had taken of the bread and the cup, Jesus said, "Now I give you a new commandment. You are to love one another, just as I have loved you. If you love one another, all men will know by this that you are my disciples."

After they had sung a hymn, they went out into the dark deserted streets of Jerusalem and made their way toward the Mount of Olives. As they walked along, Jesus said to them, "This night you will all turn away from me, for it is written, 'I will smite the shepherd, and the sheep of the flock will be scattered.' But after I am raised from the dead, I will go before you into Galilee."

Simon Peter then grabbed Jesus by the arm and declared, "Even if all the others turn away from you, I never will!"

"Oh, Peter, Peter," Jesus said, shaking his head, "before the cock crows this day, you will already have denied three times that you even know me."

"Surely not, Lord," Peter objected.

Jesus gave a wistful nod of his head and said, "Let not your heart be troubled. You believe in God; believe also in me. In my Father's house are many rooms. If it were not so, I would have told you. I am going there to prepare a place for you. And if I go and prepare a place for you, I will come again and receive you to myself, that where I am, there you may be also."

Thomas said to Jesus, "Lord, we don't know where you are going—so how can we know the way?"

"I am the way, the truth, and the life," Jesus answered. "No one can come to the Father except through me. If you really and truly

---

[37] Also called the Eucharist or Holy Communion.

knew me, you would know my Father as well. From this time on, you do know him and have seen him."

"Lord," said Phillip, "show us the Father, and that will be all we need."

"Have I been with you for so long a time," asked Jesus, "and yet you do not know me, Phillip? He who has seen me has seen the Father. Do you not believe that I am in the Father and the Father is in me? The words I say to you I do not speak on my own authority; but the Father, dwelling in me, is performing His works."

Jesus led his disciples through the familiar streets of Jerusalem, past the Lower Pool and toward the Fountain Gate. As they walked, Jesus gathered his friends around him and said, "Do not grieve for me when I am gone, for I will ask the Father to give you another Comforter to be with you forever—the Spirit of Truth, whom the world cannot receive, because it does not recognize him or know him. This Comforter—the Holy Spirit whom the Father will send to you in my name—will teach you all things, will bring to your remembrance all that I have told you, and will give you a deep inner peace that surpasses all understanding."

"Why must you leave us, Master?" asked John. "I do not understand how we can have a deep inner peace if you are not with us."

"Peace I leave with you; my peace I give to you. Not as the world gives do I give to you," Jesus responded. "Let not your heart be troubled, neither let it be afraid. You have heard me say that I am going away, but I will also be coming back to you. I have told you this before it happens so that when it takes place, you may have faith."

As they walked along the Kidron Valley that separated the temple from the Mount of Olives, Jesus pointed toward the large sculpture of a vine that adorned the temple, and declared to his disciples, "I am the true vine, and my Father is the vinedresser. Every branch in me that does not bear fruit, he trims away; and every branch that bears fruit, he prunes, that it may yield even more fruit. Already, you have been pruned by the teaching I have given you. Abide in me, and I will abide in you. Just as the branch cannot bear fruit by itself without continuing in the vine, neither can you produce spiritual fruit if you are severed from me. I am the vine, and you are the branches. Whoever abides in me, and I in him, is the one who will bear abundant fruit.

"If a man does not abide in me, he is cast forth as a severed branch and withers; such branches are gathered up and thrown into the fire and burned. If you abide in me and my words abide in you, ask whatever you wish and it will be done for you. As you bear abundant fruit, my Father will be glorified, and you will truly be my disciples."

Jesus led them across a bridge spanning the stream at the bottom of the valley and began climbing the Mount of Olives on the other side. He paused, looked intently at his disciples for a moment, and then smiled as he said, "As the Father has loved me, so have I loved you. Continue in my love. If you keep my commandments, you will continue in my love, just as I have kept my Father's commandments and continue in his love. I have told you these things so that you may share my joy, and that your joy may be complete. If you love me, you will keep my commandments. This is my commandment, that you love one another as I have loved you. Greater love has no man than that he lay down his life for his friends. You are my friends if you do what I command you—and I command you to love one another."

Jesus then turned and continued climbing up the Mount of Olives. As he walked, he continued talking, and his friends gathered closely around him to hear his words. "I am telling you all these things so that you will not go astray when they happen. The authorities will put you out of the synagogue. In fact, a time is coming when anyone who kills my followers will think he is offering a service to God. They will do such things because they do not really know God, even though they think they do. I have told you this so that when the time comes you will remember that I warned you."

Then Jesus came with his disciples to a place called Gethsemane, a garden and olive grove on the Mount of Olives where Jesus had gone in the past to pray. He said to his disciples, "Sit here, while I go over there and pray."

Taking with him his three closest disciples,[38] Jesus told them, "Stay here and keep watch with me." Then he walked a little farther, fell on his face, and fervently prayed, "My soul is very sorrowful, even to death. Father, I know you can do all things. Therefore, if it is possible—if there is any other way by which my mission can be accomplished—please let this cup pass from me.

"I have seen men who have been nailed to crosses. I have heard their cries and curses as they hang suspended between heaven and earth. But even worse is the prospect of taking on the sins of the world. I fear the cup of judgment. I shudder at the thought of being separated from you as part of that judgment. If that can be avoided, please let it be so. Nevertheless, it is not as I will, but rather your will that shall be done." Jesus' prayer was so extremely intense that bloody sweat appeared on his brow.[39]

---

[38] Peter, James and John.

[39] This rather rare phenomenon, known as hematidrosis, occurs in cases of extreme psychic stress that causes the body to release chemicals that break down capillaries in the sweat glands, which then rupture and mix with sweat; hematidrosis also makes a person feel weak and dehydrated, and causes the skin to become fragile, tender, and extremely sensitive.

When Jesus returned to the three disciples, he found that they were asleep.

"What?" Jesus remarked. "Could you not keep watch with me for even an hour? Watch and pray that you may not enter into temptation. The spirit indeed is willing, but the flesh is weak."

Jesus knew how weak the flesh would be. He knew that his disciples would flee in terror when the soldiers came to take him away. This would be the last time he would be with these men who had lived and worked with him these past three years before they abandoned him. Yet he did not spend his time crying with them or even giving final instructions. Instead, he prayed for them.

"I pray for these men. Holy Father, protect them by the power of your name—the name you gave me—so that they may be one as we are one. I pray also for those who will believe in me through their message, that all of them may be one, Father, just as you are in me and I am in you. May they be brought to complete unity to let the world know that you sent me and have loved them even as you have loved me."

By the time Jesus finished praying, he had received the answer to his prayers. He had asked if there was any other way to successfully complete his mission. Now he knew there was no other way. God loved humanity—even with all its shortcomings, pride and sin— enough to take the sins of the world onto himself, become the perfect sacrifice for those sins, and complete his mission of redemption and love.

The Sanhedrin

A large group of men bearing torches and armed with swords and clubs climbed up the limestone ridge toward Gethsemane. Judas Iscariot, who led the group, walked straight to Jesus, and said "Hail, Master!" Judas placed his right hand on Jesus' shoulder and kissed him on his cheek.

"Friend," said Jesus, "what brings you here?"

The armed detachment surrounded Jesus and grabbed him roughly. Simon Peter drew his sword and attempted to defend his master. Peter swung his sword mightily at Malchus, the High Priest's servant. Malchus dodged, but the sword cut off his right ear. Malchus made a startled cry and clutched his head. Blood oozed through his fingers. The soldiers holding Jesus released him as they turned toward Peter and drew their swords.

"Put away your sword," Jesus said to Peter, "for all who take up the sword will die by the sword." Jesus then picked up Malchus' ear, placed it back where it belonged, and instantly healed the wound. "Don't you realize that I could appeal to my Father, and he would immediately send me more than twelve legions of angels?" Jesus asked Peter. "But if I were to do that, how would the scriptures be fulfilled or my mission be accomplished? Shall I not drink the cup which my Father has given me? Though the way may be hard and painful, I must complete my mission."

Jesus turned and said to the elders and officers of the temple guard, "Have you come out with swords and clubs to capture me as if I were a robber? Day after day I sat in the temple teaching, and you did not seize me. Why do you do so now under cover of darkness?"

Peter, who had been backing up while Jesus was talking, turned and ran from the garden, followed closely by the other disciples, who ran for their lives. One of the soldiers grabbed hold of the robe worn by a young man named Mark who had been following the disciples. Mark twisted out of his robe and ran from the scene unclothed.

The band of soldiers bound Jesus and led him up the slope between the Upper City and the Tyropean to the Palace of Annas, the former high priest and father-in-law of Caiaphas, the current high priest. Annas then questioned Jesus about his disciples and his teaching.

"I have spoken openly to the world," replied Jesus. "I have continually taught in synagogues and in the temple, where all the Jews gather together, and I have said nothing in secret. Why ask me these questions? Ask those who have heard me what I told them, for they know what I have said."

Then one of the officers standing by him slapped Jesus' face with the palm of his hand and said, "Is that the way you answer the high priest?"

"If I have said anything wrong," replied Jesus, "bear witness to the wrong. But if I have answered correctly, why do you violate Jewish law by striking me?"

*****

131

In the early morning about an hour or two after midnight, Annas had Jesus bound again and sent to Caiaphas at the palace of the high priest. Caiaphas had called an emergency meeting of the Great Sanhedrin, the Grand Council of the Jewish people. Although the Sanhedrin was composed of seventy-one members who were appointed for life, the court could conduct business as long as it had a quorum of at least twenty-three members. The court sat in a semicircle with two clerks before them to record testimony and votes. Jesus and Caiaphas stood before the assembled Sanhedrin.

Then the chief priests and the whole council attempted to find witnesses who would testify against Jesus. Although they found several who were willing to testify, the witnesses' stories did not agree with one another on key points. The closest they could come was that two witnesses claimed that Jesus had said he could destroy the Temple of God and then rebuild it in three days—but even they contradicted each other on minor points.[40]

The high priest then said to Jesus, "Have you no answer to offer? What is this that these men are testifying against you?"

Jesus, however, remained silent and did not answer.

Caiaphas then said to Jesus, "I charge you on oath by the living God to tell us whether you are the Messiah, the Son of God." When a question was phrased in that manner to a loyal Jew, it was an offense not to answer.

"I AM," replied Jesus. "Hereafter, I tell you, you will see the Son of Man seated at the right hand of the Almighty and coming on the clouds of heaven."

---

[40]Under Jewish law, such contradictions could invalidate the witnesses' testimony.

The high priest dramatically tore his robes and said, "He has spoken blasphemy! What further need have we of witnesses? You have heard the blasphemy. What is your decision?"

"Death!" replied the council. "He deserves death!" Then they spat in Jesus' face and struck him, saying, "Prophesy to us, Messiah! What is the name of the man who hit you?"

Jesus, however, did not respond to the attacks. Instead, he merely looked sorrowfully at the religious leaders, sighed and shook his head.

Meanwhile, Simon Peter had followed Jesus, though from a great distance. Peter entered the courtyard of the high priest's palace and sat down among the guards to await the outcome of Jesus' trial.

While Peter was sitting in the courtyard, a maid came up to him and said, "You were with Jesus, the Galilean, weren't you?"

"I don't know what you are talking about," Peter replied as he quickly stood up and looked around fearfully. He left the courtyard and went out onto the porch, where another maid pointed at him and told the bystanders, "This man was with Jesus, the Nazarene."

Again Peter denied it, adding with an oath, "I swear I don't know the man!"

Although Peter attempted to stand in the shadows away from other people, it was not long before several guards and bystanders surrounded Peter and said, "You are definitely one of Jesus' Galilean followers. Your accent gives you away."

Peter began to curse and to swear that he didn't know the man. While he was still speaking, a rooster crowed—and Peter remembered Jesus telling him, "Before the cock crows this day, you will already have denied three times that you even know me." To make matters worse, when Peter looked around to see if anyone else was watching him, he saw Jesus looking sorrowfully at him while being led from one of the rooms.

The sudden realization that he had failed as a disciple hit Peter like a thunderbolt. He prided himself on his loyalty and love for Jesus, whom he considered to be his Lord and Master. Worse, he had loudly and proudly proclaimed that even if everyone else deserted Jesus, he would stand firm. After all, he was Peter, the rock. His faith would not waiver. But instead of standing tall, he had fallen short. The very thing he had sworn he would never do was exactly what he had just done. He had let his Master down. He had let the disciples down. He had failed to live up to even his own standards for himself. Instead of being the leader he had claimed to be, Peter had failed miserably. He stumbled from the palace, weeping bitterly.

Peter was so blinded by his tears that he did not notice the two men who passed him as they entered the courtyard he had just vacated. Both men wore garments with the wide fringes that indicated they were Pharisees, and both wore the headdresses that marked them as being members of the Sanhedrin. Both men walked briskly to the chamber in which the trial of Jesus had taken place.

"What is going on in here?" demanded one of the men.

"Oh, Nicodemus, Nicodemus," responded Matthias. "The high priest called an emergency meeting of the Sanhedrin."

"Why were we not notified of the meeting?" Nicodemus asked.

"Because of the emergency nature of the meeting, there was not time for everyone to be contacted," Matthias answered. "It would have taken too long to get word to Joseph in Arimathea, for example," he added, glancing at the second man.

"Not too long," Joseph commented, "since I was spending the night at Nicodemus' house. If you had contacted him, you would also have reached me."

"Well, it wasn't really necessary," Matthias said. "We already had more than the twenty-three members necessary to conduct a trial."

"A trial?" Joseph asked. "A trial of whom?"

"Why, a trial of Jesus of Nazareth. He admitted under oath that he was the Messiah, the Son of God. The Sanhedrin naturally found him guilty of blasphemy and has determined that he deserves to be put to death."

"A trial *at night—during the Passover?*" Nicodemus asked incredulously. "That is highly illegal!"

"Oh, you worry too much, Nicodemus. If it had really been illegal, I am sure neither the high priest nor the council would have done it. However, what's done is done. Even now Jesus is being led to Pontius Pilate to be charged according to Roman law." Matthias then smiled benignly and turned away.

Sensing that his friend was about to explode in wrathful fury, Joseph took Nicodemus by the arm and quietly whispered in his ear, "Before you say anything else, look around you and observe who is here. Only those members of the Sanhedrin who are committed to the high priests' opposition to Jesus are present. Apparently none of the more moderate members or those who would insist that we must follow our own law were notified. We would have had no notice of these proceedings ourselves if Bartholomew had not contacted us with the news that Jesus had been arrested. I suggest we quietly go to more private chambers, where we can draft a formal opposition to these proceedings."

"What good would that do?"

"We may be able to get notice to the other members of the Great Sanhedrin, and to persuade them to reconsider and to rescind the findings of this illegal trial. Or, if that doesn't work, we may be able to present the information to the Romans or even to the people who have gathered for the Passover."

"Very well, Joseph. As you say, the group that is currently assembled does not seem to be inclined to respect our own Jewish legal requirements. However, it may be prudent to set these matters out for others to consider."

When the two men had found a private chamber well removed from the others, Joseph began taking notes. Nicodemus paced back and forth as he collected his thoughts.

"First," said Nicodemus, "our own Jewish law requires that there can be no trials during the Passover, during the night, or on the eve of the Sabbath. All of those requirements have been violated. Further, it appears that the high priests acted as both prosecutors and as judges, which is highly improper. Our law does not allow any man who is concerned or interested in a matter under adjudication to even sit on the court—much less to act as prosecutor or judge."

"Matthias said Jesus' conviction was based upon his own sworn testimony," Joseph said. "Isn't that also irregular?"

"Right you are, Joseph. Our law does not permit forced self-incrimination, nor does it allow a person to be condemned merely on his own testimony.

"It also appears that they conducted this 'trial' as a capital case," Nicodemus continued. "Our law does not allow a capital case to be tried in one sitting; it must carry over to a second day in order to accomplish the rules of justice."

Nicodemus paused to allow Joseph to catch up with his notes and to flex his hand. When Joseph again picked up his stylus, Nicodemus continued, "Furthermore, if the court votes for conviction, the court must adjourn without passing sentence. Only after it has reconvened the following day and the evidence is again reviewed may another vote be taken and sentence be passed."

"Is that the reason we are forbidden to conduct a criminal trial on the day preceding the Sabbath?" Joseph asked.

"Yes," replied Nicodemus, "since the follow-up trial could not be had on that day. There were additional irregularities as well. According to Bartholomew, the arrest of Jesus was apparently brought about through the actions of a traitor who had been hired by the high priests or possibly by the court that would be passing judgment on Jesus. The Sanhedrin does not have authority to instigate charges, but is only supposed to investigate charges brought before it. Yet in this instance the court itself formulated the charges. Caiaphas presented the charges and served as prosecutor—another violation—even though as high priest he was also the presiding judge."

"I don't remember having any prior trials here at the home of the high priest," Joseph commented.

"Good point, Joseph. This night-time 'trial' was conducted at the high priest's palace rather than in the *Liscat Haggazith*[41]. Jewish law requires that there be an exhaustive search into the facts presented by any witnesses, but apparently Jesus was permitted no defense. There were probably other irregularities or illegalities that we might have noted had we been present, but this partial assembly of the Sanhedrin was apparently carefully chosen to validate the high priest's predetermined verdict rather than to conduct a trial according to Jewish laws of justice."

---

[41] The hall of polished stone where the Sanhedrin was supposed to conduct its trials and deliberations

Pilate

Shortly after daybreak on the fourteenth day of Nisan in the year 3790[42], the chief priests and elders delivered Jesus to Pontius Pilate, the Roman governor of Judea. After Herod the Great died and his son Archelaus was banished, Rome had appointed a series of governors to rule over Judea. Pilate was Rome's military procurator, and his ultimate responsibility was to the emperor himself.

Although Pilate normally stayed at his official residence in Caesarea, it was his custom to go to Jerusalem during Passover in order to quell any uprisings that might occur. While in Jerusalem, Pilate stayed at the Praetorium, the former palace of Herod the Great that was located on high ground in the northwestern portion of the Upper City, the newer portion of Jerusalem where most of the homes of wealthier citizens were located.

The chief priests and elders did not actually enter the Praetorium, since entering such a Gentile structure could cause them to be ceremonially unclean or defiled, which would mean they would be unable to partake of the Passover. Although it galled Pilate to leave the Roman fortress in order to meet with men he considered to be religious fanatics, he was nevertheless enough of a political realist to follow the most expedient course of action and do what had to be

---

[42] i.e., April 7, 30.

done. He therefore went out to the Jewish religious leaders and asked, "What charge do you bring against this man?"

"If he were not a criminal," they replied, "we would not have handed him over to you."

Pilate examined the accused with the keen eyes of a trained soldier. The man before him had no weapons and apparently no confederates or accomplices. The tall, thin governor had seen many criminals and insurrectionists and prided himself on being a good judge of character. This man did not appear to be a vicious troublemaker, though he did have an aura of authority about him.

"Take him and judge him according to your own law," Pilate said dismissively.

"We are not allowed to put anyone to death," replied Caiaphas, who then accused Jesus of several crimes: "We found this man perverting our nation and forbidding people to pay taxes to Caesar, saying that he himself is the Messiah, the king of the Jews.[43]"

Since these were potentially serious charges that Pilate could not safely ignore, and since there was something about the accused man's bearing that was both strange and compelling, he decided to

---

[43] The Sanhedrin had convicted Jesus of blasphemy (claiming to be God or making oneself equal to God) rather than perverting the nation, forbidding people to pay taxes to Caesar, or claiming to be a king. Although blasphemy was an offense that was punishable by death under Jewish law, and although the Sanhedrin had the legal right to pronounce the death sentence, the Romans had restricted that right when they conquered Palestine. The Romans reserved for themselves the right to carry out a death sentence for all offenses other than threatening the sanctity of the Jewish temple. Since the Jewish leaders had been unable to find Jesus guilty of threatening to destroy the temple, control over Jesus was surrendered to the Romans--and the accused had to be found guilty of a capital offense according to Roman law. Indeed, Rome had removed Annas from his office as high priest because he had violated that restriction. Thus, when the Jewish religious authorities turned Jesus over to Pilate for sentencing, they did not say he had been found guilty of blasphemy, which would not have concerned the Romans, but rather claimed that he was guilty of committing treason, sedition, and other related offenses.

examine the prisoner more fully, but away from the Jews who were seeking the man's death. Pilate went back into the Praetorium and had Jesus brought to him. He studied Jesus for a few moments and then remarked sarcastically, "*You* are the King of the Jews?"

"Are you saying this of your own accord?" replied Jesus. "Or did others say this to you about me?"

"Am I a Jew?" snapped Pilate. "Your own nation and the chief priests have handed you over to me. What have you done?"

A slight smile tickled the corners of Jesus' mouth. *What had he done?* Over the past three years he had primarily spent his waking hours preaching, teaching, healing and helping people. When asked a similar question by messengers from John the Baptist, Jesus had replied, "The blind receive their sight, the lame walk, lepers are cleansed, the deaf hear, the dead are raised up to life again, and the poor have the gospel preached unto them."

True, those were all important accomplishments—but they would probably hold little interest for Pilate. Jesus therefore responded, "My kingdom is not of this world. If my kingdom were of this world, my servants would have fought to keep me from being handed over to the Jews. But my authority as king is not of earthly origin."

"Are you indeed a king?" Pilate asked.

"You are right in saying that I am a king," replied Jesus. "For this purpose I was born, and for this cause I have come into the world, to bear witness to the truth. Those who love the truth listen to my voice."

"What is truth?" muttered Pilate to himself. If Jesus' kingdom was not of this world, it would not be in conflict with Caesar's empire. Pilate had heard enough to confirm his initial conclusion that this man was harmless. He then went out to the Jews and announced, "I do not find this man guilty of any crime." Pilate's public verdict that

Jesus was not guilty angered the Jewish religious leaders, who then began to accuse Jesus of many other things in an effort to get Pilate to reconsider.

"Have you no answer to offer?" Pilate asked Jesus. "Didn't you notice how many charges they have brought against you?"

But Jesus made no reply, which astonished Pilate.

The chief priest then grew more insistent, saying, "This man has been stirring up the people with his teachings, causing disturbances all the way from where he started in Galilee to here."

"Is he a Galilean?" asked Pilate.

"He is," Caiaphas answered.

Pilate turned to his steward and commanded, "Have a detachment of soldiers take the prisoner to Herod Antipas.[44] He's staying at the Palace of the Maccabees here in Jerusalem during the Passover."

When Herod Antipas was informed that Roman soldiers had brought Jesus of Nazareth to him, he responded, "Ah, excellent. I have heard much about him and am glad to finally see him in person."

Turning to his guests, Herod announced, "We may have a chance for better entertainment than these poor jugglers have provided. I have just been informed that the Romans have brought me Jesus of Nazareth. Perhaps he will show us one of his famous miracles."

Flanked by two guards, Jesus was brought before Herod Antipas, who studied him for about a minute before remarking, "So you are the famous miracle man of Galilee."

Jesus merely looked at Herod without responding.

---

[44] Galilee was in Herod Antipas' jurisdiction.

"Is it true you raised people from the dead and fed thousands of people with very little food?"

Jesus made no response.

"At least Moses put on a show for Pharaoh. Can't you do the same for us?"

No response.

A commotion signaled the arrival of the chief priests and scribes, who demanded to be taken to Herod.

"Sire," said Caiaphas, "this man is a threat to your throne, since he claims to be a king."

"A king?" chuckled Herod. "Him?"

"Yes, Sire. He claims to be the Messiah spoken of by the prophets."

Turning back toward Jesus, Herod remarked, "You heard the priest. What have you to say in your defense?"

Again Jesus said nothing.

"He also encouraged people not to pay their taxes!" added Matthias.

"No taxes?" Herod quipped to his guests. "Now this is really getting serious!"

Still Jesus made no response.

After silently watching Jesus for a couple of minutes, Herod growled, "Say something, damn you."

No response.

"Maybe what I need is another miracle man to make this first one come alive and say or do something."

Jesus continued standing respectfully in front of Herod without answering.

"Enough of this!" Herod declared as he summoned one of his slaves and ordered, "Fetch one of my older royal robes and bring it here."

When the slave returned with the robe, Herod Antipas ordered one of his soldiers to put it on Jesus. Herod and his guests finally had their entertainment as the soldiers gave mock allegiance to Jesus.[45] He then had Jesus returned to Pilate's custody.

Pilate called together the chief priests and rulers and said to them, "You brought this man to me as one who is misleading the people. After examining him before you, I have not found this man guilty of your charges against him. Nor did Herod, for he sent him back to me. This man has done nothing deserving of death. I will therefore give him a flogging and release him."

Thus Pilate announced a second verdict of not guilty, but this time he coupled his verdict with a sentence of flogging for the man he had just declared innocent of all charges. Pilate realized that it was because of their envy that the religious leaders had condemned Jesus, and he hoped that the sight of a bruised, bleeding and broken man would mollify the Jewish leaders enough to end the charade. Then the governor thought of another possible solution.

It was the custom of Pilate at the time of the Passover festival to release one prisoner to the Jews. Although he generally allowed the Jews to choose the prisoner, Pilate seized upon this custom as a means of getting out of his dilemma. He narrowed the choice to two men: Jesus and a murderer and insurrectionist named Barabbas. After all, he reasoned, who would not choose a great teacher over a notorious criminal?

---

[45] By mocking Jesus in the presence of the religious leaders, Herod hoped to curry their favor—but he refrained from passing sentence on a rabbi who was popular with the people and who had a reputation for being able to work mighty miracles.

But Pilate had not correctly evaluated how deeply the religious leaders feared and hated Jesus. The chief priests and elders persuaded the mob to ask for Barabbas and to demand the death of Jesus. The governor responded by saying to them again, "Which of the two do you want me to release to you?"

"Barabbas!" they answered.

"Then what shall I do with Jesus, who is called Messiah?" asked Pilate.

"Let him be crucified!" the crowd shouted.

Pilate's clever compromise had backfired. Instead of freeing himself, the governor had painted himself into a corner. Stunned and almost in a state of shock, he cried back to the people, "Why? What crime has he committed?"

But the mob shouted all the more, "Let him be crucified." The people then began chanting, "Crucify! Crucify! Crucify him!"

Pilate realized with horror that a riot was developing, which he could not afford at this stage of his career. He had been appointed to his position by Sejanus, who had become the *de facto* leader of Rome when Emperor Tiberius retired to the resort island of Capri four years earlier. But when Tiberius discovered that Sejanus was responsible for killing the emperor's son, Sejanus was executed, and his friends and political appointees were in danger of similar treatment.

Pilate, who had been both a friend and a political appointee of Sejanus, did not want Tiberius to have any excuse for ending his career … or his life. He took a basin of water and symbolically washed his hands in front of the people. "I am washing my hands of this affair," he said. "I am innocent of the blood of this just and righteous person. The responsibility is yours."

"May his blood be on us and on our children!" the people responded.

Then Pilate released Barabbas to them, and handed Jesus over to his soldiers to be whipped and crucified. Jesus was flogged with a Roman scourge[46], which consisted of leather straps into which pieces of sheep bone and metal had been woven, and weighted with lumps of lead at the tip of each thong. Stripped to the waist, Jesus was tied to a pillar in a stooping position that fully exposed his back.

Jesus arched his back in agony as the bits of bone and metal tore into his flesh. Each lash of the scourge ripped his body, lacerating both the skin and muscles. Since Jesus' skin was especially sensitive and fragile as a result of the hematidrosis he had suffered a few hours earlier in the Garden of Gethsemane, the brutal Roman flogging was especially destructive. Soon Jesus' back was a mass of quivering ribbons of bleeding flesh—and still the flogging continued. Jesus gasped with pain as one of the metal weights crashed into his ribs. The jeering soldiers who were watching cheered as the sound reverberated around the room.

The pain was so intense that Jesus found it necessary to direct all his thoughts to repeatedly muttering through clinched teeth, "Father, forgive them. Please don't hold this to their account. Forgive them. Forgive them." By the time the scourging ended after thirty-nine lashes, all of Jesus' back was totally shredded and laid open so that even his bones, sinews and bowels were exposed. His right lung had collapsed, and there was profuse bleeding into his chest cavity, and then down his legs. Jesus had lost enough blood that his body was beginning to experience hypovolemic shock.[47]

---

[46] Probably a *flagrum*, a whip with several long leather tails.

The soldiers then took the royal robe Herod had placed on Jesus as part of his mockery, and they placed it about his bleeding frame. Someone had braided a crown of thorns, and this was pressed down on Jesus' head. The sharp thorns cut into his flesh until the blood flowed freely from the wounds. The soldiers then placed a reed in Jesus' right hand, and they all kneeled down before him in mock subjection, shouting, "Hail, King of the Jews!" Then they spat on him, yanked the reed from him, and struck him on the head with it. When the soldiers finally finished mocking Jesus, they led him back to the governor.

Pilate addressed the mob one more time, saying, "Behold, I am bringing him out to you so that you may know that I find him guilty of no crime." The bruised and bleeding Jesus, still wearing the crown of thorns and royal robe, slowly shuffled out before the people. "Behold, here is the man!" said Pilate.

When the chief priests and the officers saw him, they shouted, "Crucify him! Crucify him!"

"Take him and crucify him yourselves," said Pilate, "for I do not find him guilty of any crime."

"We have a law," answered Caiaphas, "that says he should die because he claimed to be the Son of God."

When Pilate heard this, he became even more alarmed. He took Jesus back inside the Praetorium and asked him, "Who *are* you? Where did you come from?"

---

[47] Hypovolemic shock is caused by losing large amounts of blood. The victim's heart races in an effort to pump blood that isn't there; his blood pressure drops, which causes the victim to faint or collapse; his kidneys stop producing urine, and the body craves fluids to replace the lost volume of blood.

When Jesus did not answer him, Pilate said, "Aren't you going to speak to me? Don't you know that I have the authority to release you, and the authority to crucify you?"

"You would have no authority at all over me had it not been given to you from above," replied Jesus. "Therefore, he who handed me over to you is guilty of the greater sin."

Hearing this, Pilate renewed his efforts to release Jesus. Pilate first consulted with Julius, the governor's chief advisor, who gave the governor a summary of the information the Romans had collected regarding Jesus: He was a religious teacher who seemed to have unusual powers. He had fed thousands of people with virtually no food—and the reports claimed he had ended up with more food than when he had started. He had healed large numbers of people and had even restored life to several dead people. None of the soldiers or Roman spies reported any insurrection or other criminal acts worth noting with the possible exception of a notation that one of Jesus' disciples had been a Zealot prior to joining up with Jesus.

A man who can feed thousands of people with virtually no food and who can heal the suffering and misery of the masses would be a powerful ally, Pilate thought to himself. *Or a dangerous enemy … .*

Pilate reread a note he had received from his wife: "Have nothing to do with that righteous man, for last night I suffered greatly in a dream because of him." *What is it about this man that even causes my wife to have disturbing dreams? I wish it were that simple to just have nothing to do with this entire affair. A religious leader with unusual powers … . What if he actually is the son of the Jews' God?*

Pilate next met with Odaenathus, a Roman attorney hired by Joseph of Arimathea. Although Odaenathus admitted that as military governor, Pilate was not required to follow particular rules and forms of law, he pointed out that Pilate also had the right and power to apply either the law of the forum[48] or the law of the community.[49]

After presenting to Pilate the ways the members of the Sanhedrin had broken their own Jewish law in their trial of Jesus, Odaenathus suggested that Pilate follow the criminal procedure generally used in capital cases tried in Rome. This would require an initial hearing to be held to determine which prosecutor should present the case, and to review the charges against the accused.

If it was determined that there was enough evidence against the accused to warrant a trial, an indictment would be issued and presented to the tribunal, which would then set a date for the trial. As Odaenathus pointed out, this would allow the governor to get beyond the Passover crowds and the current mob that was obviously being controlled by the jealous Jewish religious leaders. The trial could even be held in a site more likely to produce a just result than in Jerusalem.

Pilate listened and privately agreed. When he attempted to implement that course of action, however, Caiaphas shouted, "You are not a friend of Caesar! Everyone who sets himself up as a king proclaims treason against Caesar."

The other priests took up the chant of "You're not a friend of Caesar."

Just as a card shark might save back an "ace in the hole" or the controlling trump card so that it could be used when needed in the decisive moment, so had the Jewish religious leaders reserved their strongest argument or threat for this moment. "A friend of Caesar" was a title bestowed upon those who acted in the emperor's best interests. Thus, by suggesting that Pilate would not be loyal to

---

[48] In this case, Roman law.
[49] Jewish law.

148

Caesar if he either released Jesus or failed to crucify him, they were threatening to report Pilate's actions to Tiberius Caesar, who had a reputation for sometimes reacting impulsively rather than considering all the facts, evidence and context.

The religious leaders had successfully appealed to Rome previously, and the memory of Tiberius' wrath on those occasions still burned in Pilate's mind. He knew his own life could be endangered if Tiberius Caesar learned that his governor had refused to execute a man who claimed to be a *king* in opposition to Caesar's claims as emperor. When Pilate heard these words, he brought Jesus out and sat down on the cobalt blue curule judgment seat at a place called The Pavement, which was an elevated platform of stone on which the *bema*[50] rested. Pilate said to the Jews, "Behold, your king!"

"Away with him; away with him; crucify him!" shouted the angry mob, jabbing and shaking their fists in the air.

"Shall I crucify your king?" asked Pilate.

"We have no king but Caesar," answered Caiaphas. The mob echoed his words.

Then Pilate summoned Longinus, the centurion in charge of the crucifixion detail of soldiers from the famous Roman Twelfth Legion, and Longinus led Jesus away.

Judas Iscariot had been watching from the shadows as the drama unfolded. He had seen the farce of a trial, watched Pilate vainly seek some way to free Jesus without inciting a riot, and listened as sentence was ultimately passed.

The scene in the Garden of Gethsemane kept replaying itself in Judas' mind. When he had greeted Jesus with a kiss, Jesus had gently

---

[50] The judgment seat.

asked him, "Friend, what brings you here?" Jesus' sorrowful eyes seemed to be asking, "Friend, why have you done this?"

Why had he done it, anyway? At the time it had seemed to make sense to Judas. He had hoped to force the Rabbi's hand—force him to finally take the decisive action needed to declare himself as the long awaited Messiah and establish his everlasting kingdom on earth. After all, any man who had the power to multiply food to feed the multitudes, to heal the sick and dying, to effortlessly control the storms and forces of nature, and even to raise the dead back to life again could surely have the power to overcome the Romans. He undoubtedly had the power to deflect enemy arrows, to feed and heal his troops, and even to restore life to those who fell in battle. His army would be invincible.

Jesus, however, seemed reluctant to take that decisive step. True, he had revealed himself as being the Messiah—but only to his disciples or in other private conversations. What was needed was something to ignite the spark. After Lazarus' resurrection, the witnesses were ready to proclaim Jesus as the promised Messiah and to follow him wherever he would lead them—but Jesus had merely disappeared into the house.

Judas had thought long and hard about what it would take to get Jesus to publicly declare himself as the Messiah. Judas eventually concluded that his most promising option would be to turn Jesus over to the jealous Jewish religious leaders. Granted, there were some risks involved, but Judas believed that the masses that had flocked to Jesus on Palm Sunday would surely rally to his defense and would unite behind Jesus in a popular groundswell of support that would proclaim Jesus as the long-awaited Messiah who would deliver his people from Roman oppression.

But Judas' plan had gone horribly wrong. Instead of uniting behind Jesus, the mob had united against him. Instead of overthrowing the Roman oppressors, Jesus was about to be crucified by them. And most maddening of all was that Jesus was allowing it to happen! He did not summon the armies of heaven or even call upon the forces of nature. Time and again Judas had seen Jesus restore dead people to life. Now this one who had power over life and death was willingly walking to his own death. *Like a lamb being led to be slaughtered,* thought Judas. *It's maddening! Pointless! Insane!*

Judas bitterly turned from the scene and absentmindedly caressed the purse containing the thirty pieces of silver given to him by the jealous religious leaders. When he had received the money, Judas had thought of it as a bonus for ingeniously prompting the Rabbi to lead the movement that would overthrow the Roman dogs. Now the coins mocked him each time he heard them jingle. Judas had betrayed the Rabbi for the price of a slave! Betrayed! Only a trusted friend could truly betray someone. Judas had violated his Master's trust. What use had he for blood money?

Judas was filled with remorse and brought back the thirty pieces of silver to the priests and elders at the temple. Judas kneeled down before them, held out the money, and said, "I have sinned by betraying innocent blood."

"What is that to us?" Annas replied. "That is your affair."

Judas looked at the priests through eyes devoid of any hope. The priests were caretakers of an empty religion also devoid of hope and meaning. They went through an empty charade of rituals and pompous ceremonies. *For what purpose? What meaning? The only man who had ever given meaning to life was the one Judas had betrayed.* Well, Jesus had warned that it would have been better for the man who betrayed him if he had never been born. How true were those words—and how they now cut Judas to the bone.

Judas threw the silver down in the courtyard[51] and ran away, howling his dismay like a madman. Perhaps he was a madman. It *would* have been better if he had never been born. Not only was he a failure, but he was also a traitor to his Master. If anyone ever remembered Jesus in the future, they very likely would also remember that he had been betrayed by Judas Iscariot. That was not the way Judas wanted to be remembered, but there was nothing he could do now to rectify his actions.

Judas stumbled blindly down the dusty streets of Jerusalem. Where could he go? Certainly not back to the disciples with whom he had lived these past three years. He couldn't even return to his family after what he had done. Instead of being honored as the one who helped lead Israel's successful revolt against the Roman dogs, he had brought shame, disgrace and dishonor upon himself and his family. Better if he had never been born!

Never been born; maybe that was the answer. Life had lost its purpose and its meaning. Perhaps it was time to face the final futility—or the futile finality. Judas bought some rope and trudged eastward down a dirty Jerusalem street.

His body was later found hanging from the limbs of a tree just outside Jerusalem.

---

[51] The priests picked up the silver coins and commented, "It is unlawful to put this into the temple treasury, since it is the price of blood." After discussing their options, they eventually used the money to purchase the "potters' field"—so named because its clay was used by potters to make jars and pots—to use as a burial place for strangers and paupers. Because the land was purchased with Judas' blood money, the land became known as the Field of Blood.

Vía Dolorosa

The crucifixion detail stripped the royal robes from Jesus and put his own garments on him. Since his back had been thoroughly lacerated by the scourging, tearing the robes from his back caused his wounds to be ripped open again, which resulted in an additional loss of blood.

The soldiers placed the patibulum, or horizontal crossbar of the cross, across the nape of Jesus' neck, balanced it along both shoulders, and then tied his outstretched arms to it. Three other men had been previously condemned to be crucified, but one of those three—Barabbas—had been released to the Jewish mob by Pilate. Thus, Jesus was joined by the other two condemned men, each of whom carried his own patibulum to the place he would be executed. Four soldiers were assigned to each of the three convicts, and a contingent of Roman guards surrounded them. The entire crucifixion detail was under the command of the centurion Longinus. The Roman guard immediately in front of each condemned man carried that man's titulus, a sign on which the condemned man's name and crime were displayed. Anyone watching the procession would therefore know what crime the man had been convicted of committing. Later, the titulus would be attached to the top of the convict's cross.

Keeping pace with the soldiers was a group of women. Although their faces were largely hidden by veils, their grief could not be hidden. Some cried, while others prayed or moaned. One woman, who was clutching a small child, kept repeating over and over to anyone near enough to hear her, "How can they kill the man who healed my child?"

As the procession moved from the Praetorium along the Via Dolorosa toward the place where the crucifixion would take place, Jesus stumbled and fell. Since his arms were tied to the crossbar he carried, Jesus could not break his fall. His face slammed against the rough uneven stones paving the street. Blood trickled down Jesus' face from lacerations on his right cheek. One of the soldiers lashed him severely with a scourge. Longinus, however, directed two other soldiers to help lift the patibulum so that Jesus could stand under the load. As Jesus struggled to his feet, a middle-aged man rushed to his side and gave him a gourd of water before being knocked backward by one of the soldiers.

"What do you think you are doing?" shouted the Roman to the man.

"He cured my blindness," the man answered.

Twice more Jesus fell. He had lost a great deal of blood during his scourging and was in much worse condition than the other two convicts. The third time he fell, it was obvious to Longinus that the rabbi had lost too much blood to be able to continue carrying the patibulum—which weighed over a hundred pounds—by himself. Looking around, the centurion saw a man in the crowd who appeared to be rather strong, and whose dress indicated he was probably a Gentile.

"You," he said to the man. "Pick up that crossbar and carry it for this man."

"Me?" cried the stranger. "I have nothing to do with this affair. I was merely on my way into Jerusalem from Cyrene when my way was blocked by this throng of people."

"What is your name?"

"Simon. Please let me proceed on my way."

"Granted," Longinus said. "You may proceed on your way as soon as you have taken this patibulum to the top of that hill."

As two of the soldiers started toward Simon to help enforce the order, the Cyrene shrugged, handed a pack he had been carrying to one of his companions, and moved over to the place where Jesus lay. The soldiers untied the ropes that bound the patibulum to Jesus and laid it across Simon's shoulders. He then quickly carried the heavy wooden crossbar up the hill and dumped it onto the ground near the other two convicts and the rest of the soldiers. Then Simon briskly returned to his companions on the road and they proceeded into Jerusalem.

The hill where Jesus and the other two condemned men were crucified was called Golgotha.[52] It was Roman custom to perform the crucifixions outside the city walls, but close enough to both the walls and to major roads to be easily visible to large groups of people.

The vertical portion of the cross—the heavy upright wooden stipes, which would typically weigh about two hundred pounds— permanently remained at the site of execution. The crossbar would be attached to the stipes to form the cross of execution. If the executioners desired to prolong a person's death over several days, they might use ropes to tie the arms to the crossbar rather than using spikes, which would usually cause greater loss of blood and thus would hasten death. Since these three executions were being

---

[52] The Aramaic form of the Hebrew word meaning "the place of the skull." The Latin version is Calvary.

performed on the day before the Passover Sabbath, all three bodies would be required to be removed from the crosses before sundown to keep from offending Jewish religious customs and legal requirements. Therefore, all three men were nailed to their respective crosses.

The Roman soldiers attached the patibulum to the stipes, stripped Jesus' clothing from him[53], and set it aside. One of the soldiers roughly shoved Jesus to the ground, and two other soldiers positioned his body above the stipes, and then stretched out his arms above the patibulum. The fourth soldier in the detail pressed a knee against Jesus' right forearm and placed a tapered iron spike approximately six inches long next to Jesus' right wrist.

Jesus turned his head toward the man. He had once stilled a stormy sea by pointing to it with that same hand and commanding the storm to be still. That hand had pointed at Lazarus' tomb when he issued the command that raised the dead. That hand had mixed his saliva with dirt when he gave the gift of sight to a blind man. That hand had picked up a servant's ear when he healed the one who was arresting him at Gethsemane. But this time he did nothing to stop the soldier from driving the spike through his wrist between the radius and the carpal bones.[54] Instead, Jesus merely writhed with pain as the spike pierced his skin, severed his sensorimotor median nerve, impaled his flexor pollicis longus, and then anchored his arm to the wooden crossbar.

---

[53] Romans stripped crucifixion victims to heighten their sense of shame.

[54] By placing the nail between either the radius and the carpal bones or between the two rows of carpal bones, the spike would not fracture any bones and would permit the victim's skeleton to support his weight during the crucifixion. It should also be noted that people at that point in time customarily considered the wrist to be part of the hand.

After both arms had been nailed to the patibulum, both Jesus and the cross to which he was nailed were lifted up. Jesus' cry of agony mixed with the jarring thud of the cross as the stipes fell into the hole that had been prepared for it. Since Jesus' two companions had been nailed to their respective crossbars while Simon was carrying Jesus' patibulum up Golgotha, they were crucified on the shorter or lower Tau crosses, so called because they were shaped like that Greek letter (T). However, the cross in the center was the higher immissa or Latin cross. After Jesus was hanging from his cross, his ankles were squeezed sideways into a small U-shaped wooden block, which was then nailed to the stipes in such a manner that the nails were driven through Jesus' heels, securing the block to the cross. The soldiers then drove wedges between the beam and the sides of the hole to keep the cross fully upright.

After the nailing had been completed, the titulus was attached to the cross right above the condemned man's head. Pilate had instructed that Jesus' titulus should be inscribed in Hebrew, Latin and Greek as "Jesus of Nazareth, the King of the Jews." When the chief priests saw the titulus, they complained bitterly to Pilate, "Do not write 'The King of the Jews'; Instead, write 'This man said, "I am King of the Jews."'"

Pilate answered forcefully, "What I have written, I have written," and refused to change the wording on Jesus' titulus. Although the words correctly stated the charge for which Jesus was being executed, Pilate may have intended the message to mock the jealous Jewish leaders or to warn other persons with kingly aspirations of Rome's likely response. In any event, the message that Jesus was "King of the Jews" was conveyed in the language of Jewish religion and history, the language of Roman law and government, and the language of Greek culture.

When the soldiers had nailed Jesus to the cross, they took his garments and divided them so that each would have one item. However, since his tunic was seamless, woven in one piece from top to bottom, they decided to cast lots for it to see whose it should be.

By law, the condemned man was normally given a bitter drink of wine mixed with myrrh or gall as a mild analgesic. Jesus, however, refused to take any drug that would deaden his pain or reduce his consciousness.

Crucifixion

Longinus was intrigued by the man hanging on the center cross. It had been his duty to observe Jesus several times over the past couple of years. He had heard Jesus preach his message of forgiveness and compassion; he could probably recite verbatim what Jesus would say about God's grace and mercy. But Longinus was curious about how such platitudes would measure up against the realities of crucifixion.

The centurion was no stranger to crucifixions. He was accustomed to being cursed and reviled by men hanging on crosses. Rage, hostility and threats of retaliation were common. Even notorious murderers would claim to be innocent and would curse both their accusers and their executioners.

Jesus, however, showed none of those emotions. Granted, he did cry out in agony when the cross fell into its hole with a resounding thud—but that cry was not accompanied with the vindictive verbiage that streamed from the other two crosses.

Longinus looked at all three men. Although their arms had been stretched out in virtually straight lines when they were being nailed to their crosses, the weight of their bodies and the ripping of their flesh had caused their arms to form V positions. Both shoulders were dislocated. When Jesus' bones were ripped out of their joints, his arms stretched and were lengthened by approximately six inches.

All three men moaned at the almost unbearable pain in their wrists, and all three attempted to flex their muscles to relieve the severe cramping that knotted their forearms and the pads of their shoulders. It was plain that all three convicts were suffering, but only the two known by Longinus to be guilty of insurrection were bitterly complaining about their fate.

When the soldiers finished stabilizing the crosses by driving wedges of wood around the bases, the perimeter guards stepped back and allowed the onlookers to approach the spectacle. The mob that had been demanding Jesus' crucifixion pressed forward to get a better look at their victim. Faces leered up at the teacher who was now suspended above them. Fingers pointed to the man who had calmed raging storms but now seemed helpless and humbled. Snarling faces convulsed as they taunted him, wagged their heads, and gloated.

"Not so all-powerful now, are you, Jesus?" Matthias jeered. "You, who would destroy the temple and build it again in three days, save yourself! If you really are the Son of God, come down from the cross!"

A Pharisee named Saul hugged Matthias and exulted, "We got him! Despite everything, we finally succeeded in bringing him down." Saul then joined in the mockery by motioning toward Jesus while jeering, "He saved others, but he cannot save himself." The chief priests, scribes and elders laughed and repeated the taunt.

Caiaphas turned to his colleagues and loudly intoned, "He claimed to be the Messiah—the King of Israel! Let him now come down from the cross, and we will believe him. Since he trusts in God, let the

Lord rescue him—provided, of course, that God really cares anything about him. After all, he claimed that he was the Son of God!"

Longinus studied the faces of the men who were reviling Jesus, and then turned to look at the rabbi nailed to the cross. The difference startled the centurion. The religious leaders reminded him of a band of demons celebrating the demise of a hated enemy, while the man on the cross looked sad and sympathetic.

The crowd's jeering was so loud that only those standing near Jesus' cross heard him quietly pray, "Father, forgive them, for they know not what they do."

Longinus closely studied Jesus' face as he spoke. *I think he's serious. He really is praying for his enemies—not for their condemnation and death, but rather for their forgiveness and salvation. How often have I seen crucified men pray for their god to rain vengeance upon the heads of their enemies—but never have I heard something like this!*

If I had been convicted of a crime I didn't commit, could I pray for my accusers? If I had been nailed to a cross, could I pray for the jealous leaders who had put me there? I had heard him teaching that we should pray for our enemies, but dismissed those statements as being impractical platitudes that could never happen. But he's actually doing it!

Longinus snapped out of his thoughtful reverie as he became aware that his soldiers had joined the crowd in mocking Jesus, coming up to him and offering him vinegar, and saying, "If you really are the King of the Jews, save yourself!"

One of the criminals being executed alongside Jesus yelled to him, "Yeah, if you really are the Messiah, save yourself—and us!"

However, the other condemned man rebuked the first one by saying, "Don't you even fear God—you who are receiving the same punishment? You and I fully deserve the punishment we are getting for what we did. But this man has done nothing wrong." Then he turned as far as he could toward Jesus and pleaded, "Lord Jesus, please remember me when you come into your kingdom."

"I tell you truly," Jesus replied through lips that were cracked and swollen, "today you will be with me in paradise."

*****

Standing near the cross was a group of grieving women, including Jesus' mother. Mary thought back to Gabriel's announcement that she had been chosen by God to bear the Christ child—the promised Messiah who would save his people. She had willingly allowed herself to be used for God's mission, even though it meant people would spread rumors about her and talk about how she had been unfaithful to Joseph. When he had taken her as his wife anyway, the gossip had changed to make him a party to the shame of not waiting until marriage to be intimate with each other. When they had returned to Nazareth after Jesus' birth, the gossipers resumed making their snide remarks.

It had not been an easy life, but Mary had willingly and even joyfully done her part. However, seeing her son nailed to a cruel cross, broken and bleeding, eyes puffy and body covered with caked blood, was more than she could bear. Making it even worse were the gloating, mocking and derisive insults being hurled at her son by the people who surrounded the crosses. They were nothing but a pack of jackals!

God had promised Mary that the child she bore would be the long-anticipated Messiah who would save his people. She had always believed that God was trustworthy and kept his promises. *If that is true, then how can it end this way? Jesus never hurt anyone. He spent his entire life helping and healing, encouraging and lifting people up. Where is God's justice in allowing these jackals to treat him this way? How does this fulfill Gabriel's promise? What is the purpose? God, how can you let this happen?*

*****

Standing next to Mary was Mary Magdalene, whose life had quite literally been transformed by Jesus. Once she had vainly sought to find meaning in life by looking in all the wrong places. Because she was unusually attractive and naturally seductive, she had numerous men who showered her with attention and material possessions. But the odd thing was that the more she got what she thought she wanted, the more miserable she felt. Just when she thought life had no meaning, she met Jesus—and he almost magically rid her of the demons that were tormenting her.

Mary Magdalene had followed Jesus ever since. He was different from any other man she had ever known. Although she had initially attempted to flirt with him, Jesus seemed impervious to her seductive powers and seemed only concerned with her spiritual relationship with God. However, being around Jesus and learning from his teaching had given purpose and meaning to her life. Until now. Seeing the most wonderful person she had ever known suspended between heaven and earth on a Roman cross was causing her mind to spin out of control. Knowing that he would soon be dead was even worse. And those jeering, leering maniacs taunting Jesus really caused her blood to boil!

It just isn't right! God, where is your justice? How can you let this happen? The great physician shouldn't die; the good shepherd should still be caring for his flock. Her eyes filled with tears as she clung to Jesus' mother and to the "other" Mary—the one who was the wife of Clopas—for support. All three Marys cried, averting their

163

eyes at times because it was so painful to watch Jesus hanging in agony.

*****

When Jesus saw his mother standing near his disciple John, he said to her, "Woman, behold your son," and tilted his head toward John. Then he said to John, "Behold your mother."

John gasped as he realized the implications. Although it would have been customary for Mary's other children to look after her once Jesus was no longer able to do so, he was passing his mantle as eldest son to his beloved disciple. In so doing, Jesus was entrusting her care to John. The disciple silently nodded, signaling his willingness to take Mary into his own home and care for her.

*****

Longinus shook his head and marveled to himself, *Even as this man is struggling for breath while dying on a cross, he still is primarily concerned for the welfare of others!*

Although the pain involved in a crucifixion is quite literally excruciating,[55] the actual cause of death is a long, slow, agonizing suffocation caused by the body's inability to perform normal respiration and exhalation.[56] In order to perform anything approximating normal breathing, Jesus had to push himself upward and fight for his breath, even though such a maneuver produced searing pain. Pushing up caused the nail to tear through his foot,

---

[55] "Excruciating" is a term that means "of or from the cross."

[56] The weight of the body pulling down on the outstretched arms and shoulders locked Jesus' intercostal muscles in an inhalation position that caused him to almost be unable to exhale. Although crucifixion caused the victim's body to experience hypovolemic shock, dehydration, stress-induced heart arrhythmias, and congestive heart failure, the actual cause of death was normally asphyxiation, which occurred when the victim's exhausted body gave out and he could no longer push up for breath.

eventually locking up against the tarsal bones, and scraped his blooded and pulverized back against the coarse wood of the cross. He could then take several rapid breaths before letting his body relax as he hung by his wrists for a few moments before pushing back up again for more breath.

Beginning around noon, a strange and unnatural darkness covered the land for approximately three hours. The uncanny darkness at this time of day had a sobering effect upon the crowd. The jeers faded into silence, and the mob began to disperse.

*****

At least two of the Jewish religious leaders who watched Jesus' execution did not join in the mockery, jeering and celebrations. Rather, they stood off by themselves in stunned silence as the man they had hoped was the promised Messiah was nailed to the cross and as he slowly died.

"I really believed that he was the Messiah," said Joseph of Arimathea sorrowfully.

"I hadn't come to that conclusion," Nicodemus responded, "but I had pretty well concluded that he was the Son of God, since the evidence we found indicated that God Almighty had used a part of his own pure energy or spirit to impregnate Mary. However, if Jesus dies, that should show conclusively that he could not be partially God or even the Son of God."

"Why is that?" Joseph asked.

"Well, since God is eternal, he obviously cannot die. Therefore, if Jesus dies, he could not be God or even the Son of God."

"Couldn't the same thing be said about the Messiah?" asked Joseph. "Since the Messiah is supposed to sit on the throne of David and rule our people forever, he would have to be alive for that to occur. Thus, if he dies, he could not reign as Messiah."

"You are probably correct, Joseph. Indeed, I think you are right. Dying would show that he is not the Messiah and is not the Son of God."

"Then both of us have been mistaken about Jesus and who he really is."

"So it would seem, Joseph. So it would seem."

The two men were quiet for several minutes. Then Joseph announced, "Well, I have decided to act on the last portion of Jesus' prayer for us that night we met with him."

"What do you mean?"

"Jesus prayed that you and I would have the courage to do what was right."

"I remember—but just what do you have in mind?"

"It appears unlikely to me that any miraculous event is going to occur that will save Jesus from death on the cross. If God were going to send the armies of heaven to intervene, I don't think he would have sent this darkness that has now lasted for over an hour. No, I think Jesus is going to die. But he doesn't have to die as a common criminal whose body will be tossed on a refuse pile or burned. I have decided that what is right would be to provide a decent burial for him."

"What?" asked Nicodemus incredulously. "All this time that you were hoping or even possibly believing he was the Messiah, you've been too afraid of our comrades on the Sanhedrin to declare to anyone other than me what you thought. Now that you know he is not the Messiah, you decide to openly show your support for him by giving him a proper burial? Am I hearing you correctly?"

"It does sound crazy, doesn't it?" Joseph remarked. "Nevertheless, I am convinced that it is the right and proper thing to do."

"Let me point out something else," Nicodemus added. "In addition to possibly alienating our friends and associates among the Jewish religious hierarchy, touching a dead body will render you unclean for the entire Passover celebration—one of the most important events of our year. In fact, it will mean you would be ceremonially unclean for seven full days."

"Perhaps that is why it will take courage to do what is right in this situation."

"It's madness, man. Do you realize all the things that must be done in order to carry out such an assignment—and how little time you have to get it done?"

"Yes, I think I do know, Nicodemus. As soon as Jesus dies, I must go to Pilate and request that his body be turned over to me. I would also need to procure the long linen burial cloth as well as the spices that must be wrapped in that cloth in order to offset the smell of the decaying body."

"That's just the beginning. Where would you put the body? Remember, everything must be completed before the Sabbath begins at six o'clock this evening."

"That's the easy part. I can use my own tomb. It is only a short distance from here."

"But that is your personal tomb for you and your family. You could never use it once a convicted criminal's body has been placed inside it."

"I know, but I am convinced that this is what is right and is what needs to be done for Jesus. Will you join me?"

"I...I don't know, Joseph. You know how hard I have worked to become recognized as Israel's master teacher of the law, don't you? I could be throwing all that away by joining you in this one reckless act."

"Yes, Nicodemus, I know. As I said earlier, it would require courage to do what is right. Prayerfully consider whether such an action is also right for you. You may join me if you wish, or I will do it alone. The choice is yours. But don't delay too long. We don't have much time. I am going to go to my shipping office to round up some men to assist me. If you wish to help, then purchase the linen and burial spices. I'll be back here as soon as I gather my men. And cheer up. Perhaps God will still send a few legions of his angels to save Jesus from the cross, and none of our actions and preparations will be needed." With that, Joseph trotted back down the road that led to Jerusalem. Nicodemus sank to his knees and earnestly prayed.

*****

During this time of darkness, Jesus felt the overwhelming weight of the sins of mankind being pressed against his soul—a feeling even more horrible than the excruciating pain of physical crucifixion. Though he had never sinned, he felt the shame and disgrace of sinners. He who had never murdered, stolen, committed adultery or lied now felt the embarrassment and shame felt by murderers, thieves, adulterers and liars. Since he bore the sins of the world, he felt the collective shame of a world of sinners.

Just as agonizing for him, however, was the terrible loneliness he felt as he was separated from the sustaining presence of divine support. That was worse than the pain of the spikes, worse than the agony of pushing up to get breath, and worse than the irritation of the flies, gnats, and other insects that were attracted to the battered and bleeding bodies nailed to rough crosses.

About three o'clock in the afternoon, Jesus arched his back, straining against the spikes that held him to the cross, tilted his head upward and cried with a loud voice to heaven above, "My God, my God, why have you forsaken me?" Jesus had reached the point where he was the perfect sacrifice for a world of sinners. As if in response to his question, the darkness abated and light returned to the land.

Jesus then looked around and said, "I thirst!"

One of the soldiers took a sponge, filled it with vinegar, stuck it on a reed, and held it up to Jesus' mouth for him to drink. When Jesus had done so, he took a deep breath as he pushed up one final time, and shouted triumphantly, "*Tetelestai!*[57] It is finished! Father, into your hands I commit my spirit." Jesus then bowed his head, stopped pushing up for breath, and died.

A sudden earthquake shook the land, splitting rocks and opening tombs. Shock waves were felt in the temple. Several priests were in the temple's inner chamber[58] when they heard a loud ripping noise. As they watched, the extremely thick, elaborate and strong inner veil[59] of the temple was torn in two, from top to bottom.

"What in the world?" cried one priest.

"That's impossible!" exclaimed another. "Not even teams of oxen could pull apart that curtain!"

"Oh, my God! Look! We can see into the Holy of Holies itself," said a third priest as he sank to his knees and then fell face down on the

---

[57] *Tetelestai* was a Greek accounting term meaning that a debt had been paid in full. In this case Jesus was declaring that the debt for mankind's sin had been paid in full, the ledger had been balanced, and nothing else is required to be paid.

[58] Only priests were allowed to enter this chamber, which was known as the Holy Place.

[59] The *katapetasma* was sixty feet long, thirty feet wide, and as thick as the palm of a man's hand; it separated the Holy Place from the Holy of Holies.

floor. "Pray that we aren't struck dead for seeing what only the high priest is allowed to see—and he can only do it on the Day of Atonement."

The other priests looked at each other in alarm, and then they also quickly prostrated themselves and prayed earnestly.

*****

The centurion Longinus and his soldiers had initially been intrigued by Jesus' lack of the emotions they had come to expect at crucifixions; there was no rage, fear, anger, hostility, cursing or threats of retaliation. Instead, they witnessed Jesus' kindness and compassion as he hung on the cross—and they observed with awe the prolonged three-hour darkness during what should have been the brightest part of the day. The darkness had ended immediately before Jesus' final comments, declaration of victorious accomplishment of his mission, and death, and was followed immediately thereafter by the earthquake. Longinus knelt down and reverently exclaimed, "Surely this man really was the Son of God!"

When the people in the crowd who had gathered to see the spectacle saw what had happened, they returned home confused as to what they had witnessed—and what it all meant. Jesus' friends and the women who had followed him from Galilee stood at a distance from the crosses, but watched all these things from that vantage point.

Because the law of Moses does not allow bodies to remain on crosses on the Sabbath, the Jews had asked Pilate to have the criminals' legs broken and then have the bodies disposed of so that they would not remain hanging between heaven and earth on the Sabbath. Breaking the legs would cause almost immediate death, of course, since the victim could no longer push up for breath. The soldiers therefore broke the legs of the men crucified with Jesus.

Since Jesus was already dead, they did not break his. Nevertheless, one of the soldiers pierced Jesus' side with a spear, perforating his right lung, pericardium and heart. Blood and water immediately flowed out, satisfying the Roman soldiers that Jesus was truly dead.[60]

---

[60] Jesus' hypovolemic shock would have caused a sustained rapid heart rate, which in turn led to heart failure and resulted in the collection of fluid in the membrane around the heart and lungs, which is called pericardial effusion and pleural effusion, respectively. When the soldier's spear was pulled out of Jesus' body, the clear fluid or effusion came out, followed by a large volume of blood.

Burial

Shortly before the middle of the afternoon, Joseph returned to Golgotha with a contingent of his men. He did not see Nicodemus, but watched the events that unfolded that day. As soon as Longinus officially pronounced Jesus to be dead, Joseph and one of his servants rode into Jerusalem on horseback. He went directly to Pilate's quarters in the Praetorium and sought audience with the governor.

Pilate was shocked to see a Jewish Pharisee and member of the Great Sanhedrin in the Roman structure. "I thought you Jews couldn't enter this building without becoming defiled," Pilate remarked.

"If you grant my request, I will be worse than defiled," Joseph answered.

"Sounds interesting. What is your request?"

"Your Excellency, I request permission to take the body of Jesus of Nazareth so that it may be given a proper burial."

"Is he already dead?"

"Yes, your Excellency. You may verify his death with your crucifixion detail."

"I'll do that." Pilate turned to one of his guards and said, "Go with this man to Calvary and speak to the centurion Longinus. If Jesus is truly dead, release his body to this man. That will be one fewer corpse to dispose of. And tell Longinus that when he returns from

172

Calvary, I want a full report about both the crucifixion and the mob that demanded Jesus' execution."

When they got back to Golgotha, Longinus confirmed that Jesus was dead, and the body was removed from the cross by the Roman soldiers and granted to Joseph, who had his men transport it to Joseph's own new tomb cut in the rock in a nearby garden, and in which no one had yet been laid. Nicodemus also returned with about seventy-five pounds' weight of myrrh, aloe and similar burial spices.

They took Jesus' body and flexed and massaged his arms to relieve the rigor mortis that had fixed his arms in the V position. Then they washed his body in accordance with Jewish law and custom, bound it in linen winding cloths along with the spices, also according to the burial custom of the Jews, and laid it in Joseph's tomb. A separate napkin tied under Jesus' chin kept his mouth from opening wide as his muscles loosened.

They then rolled the large disk-shaped stone known as the Golel[61] along its curved notch so that it firmly blocked the entrance to the tomb. Jewish law required everything to be completed before sundown.[62]

The next day, the chief priests and a group of Pharisees gathered before Pilate and said, "Sir, we remember that while he was still alive, that imposter and deceiver, Jesus of Nazareth, said that he would rise again on the third day after his death. Therefore, we ask you to command that Jesus' tomb be made secure until after the

---

[61] Golel means "great stone."

[62] Not only must they complete all work prior to the Sabbath (which began at sundown), but Deuteronomy 21:22-23 says, "If a man guilty of a capital offense is put to death and his body is hung on a tree, you must not leave his body on the tree overnight. Be sure to bury him that same day, because anyone who is hung on a tree is under God's curse."

third day, lest his disciples come and steal his body away and claim to the people that he has indeed risen from the dead. If that were allowed to happen, this last fraud would be worse than any of the others."

"You shall have a guard," Pilate responded. "In addition to the guard I post, you may also use your own guard to make it as secure as you can."

Thus it was that the Jewish religious leaders—whose chief complaints about Jesus tended to be that he healed people on the Sabbath rather than observing their rules and regulations not to do any work on that day—gathered together temple guards and posted them around the tomb of Jesus ... on the Sabbath—and not just any Sabbath, but on the high day of the Passover Sabbath itself.

When the Roman guard assigned by Pilate arrived at Jesus' tomb, they first rolled aside the huge Golel that blocked the entrance. Because the stone weighed several tons and because it rested in the deep slanting groove that had been hewn out of the rock at the base of the entrance, such stones were extremely difficult to push back up the incline. Nevertheless, the soldiers did so, since they had been commanded to confirm that the body of Jesus was still there.

After the soldiers had confirmed that Jesus' body was in the tomb and that there were no other openings into the tomb, they rolled the Golel back into place and sealed the entrance by cementing it to the surrounding stone. The Roman soldiers then placed hardening clay across the stone and marked it with the seal of the emperor. Breaking such a seal would invite Roman retaliation and retribution. Then both the Roman and the Jewish temple guards took their positions around the tomb.

Sunday Morning

Early Sunday morning a great earthquake shook the land, and an angel of the Lord descended from heaven in full view of the men who had been posted around Jesus' tomb. The angel's appearance was as bright as lightning, and his garments were as white as snow. His power was obvious to the guards, for he was able to effortlessly roll back the Golel from the entrance to the tomb, even though it had been cemented and sealed the day before. The guards fell to the ground and prostrated themselves before the angel. Then, at their first opportunity, they fled.

Meanwhile, three women—Mary Magdalene, Mary the mother of James, and Salome—had purchased spices so that they might anoint the body of Jesus as a final tribute to him.

"How are we going to get past the Golel?" asked Mary Magdalene. "We aren't strong enough to move the great stone."

"There will probably be enough men nearby who can help us," answered Mary.

"Even if we are unable to move the stone, it shouldn't make that much difference," added Salome. "Nicodemus and Joseph have already used a king's ransom in spices to anoint the body. There's really not that much need for what we are doing."

"That may be true," answered Mary Magdalene, "but I feel I must do at least this much for Jesus after all he has done for me."

"Which is why we're here," nodded Salome. "I just hope we can find someone who can help us move the stone."

"Look!" exclaimed Mary. "The tomb is open."

"Someone has already rolled the stone away," said Mary Magdalene.

"Who would have done such a thing?" asked Mary. "Do you think it's safe to enter?"

"I don't know," answered Salome as she furtively looked around.

Mary Magdalene cautiously peered into the chamber and gasped, "His body is missing!"

The other two women hurried to the entrance and looked in.

"Who would take his body?" asked Salome as she turned toward Mary Magdalene—but Mary had already turned and was running away from the tomb.

"Where do you suppose she's going?" Salome asked the other Mary.

"I have no idea, but I find it strange that the grave clothes are still here even though the body is missing."

"You're right," remarked Mary. "Why would a grave robber leave the expensive linen and spices?"

Their conversation was interrupted when the angel who had rolled aside the stone suddenly appeared. "Do not be afraid," said the angel to the frightened women. "You are looking for Jesus of Nazareth, who was crucified. He has risen and is not here. See, here is the place where they had laid him," and the angel pointed to the linen cloths that had encased Jesus' body. "Now go and tell his disciples and Peter that he will go ahead of you into Galilee, and you will see him there, as he has told you."

When the women remained where they were standing, two other angels in dazzling garments appeared before them and asked them,

"Why are you seeking the living among the dead? He is not here, but has risen. Remember how he told you, while he was still in Galilee, that the Son of Man must be delivered into the hands of sinful men and be crucified, but that on the third day he would rise from the dead?"

The women then remembered the words of Jesus, and they quickly departed from the tomb with both fear and great joy. They sought out the disciples to tell them the news, but the disciples they found did not believe them.

While the other women were encountering the angels at Jesus' tomb, Mary Magdalene ran to the house where Simon Peter and John were staying. When she informed them that someone had taken Jesus' body from the tomb, both men rushed to the tomb to see for themselves.

John, who was younger than Peter, reached the opening first. He looked inside and saw that the only items in the tomb were the long winding linen cloth that had been wrapped around Jesus' body and the smaller cloth which had been wrapped around his head. The sickly sweet smell of burial spices gave mute testimony that they were also present in the tomb.

Then Simon Peter arrived, went inside the tomb, and also observed the cloths and spices. "Why would any grave robber take a dead body and leave the expensive linen and spices?" Peter asked. "For that matter, wouldn't it have been faster and easier just to scoop up everything together instead of leaving these items behind?"

"I don't think the Master's body was taken," John replied. "The long linen cloths are not unwound. Rather, they are still wound around—but the body itself is missing. It's as if the body has passed through the cloth. I think the Master may have risen from the dead."

177

Peter looked again at the grave cloths. The eight-foot long linen cloths were still wrapped around in a shape that resembled a human body. Although the cocoon formed by the linen wrappings and the herbs and spices was still intact, it was partially deflated because the body it had encased was no longer there.

"I realize the Lord had power to raise others from the dead," Peter said. "But this time he was himself dead. Once he died, he would have had no power to raise himself."

"Perhaps God resurrected him," John said. "However, whatever happened, we probably shouldn't remain here, lest we be accused of stealing the body."

"Right!" Peter nodded. The two men returned to the home where they had been staying and wondered greatly about what had happened.

By the time Mary Magdalene returned to the tomb, both Peter and John had departed. Mary wandered around the outside of the tomb, weeping bitterly. She eventually went to the entrance of the tomb and peered inside as she wept. To her surprise, she saw two angels in white sitting where the body of Jesus had lain. "Woman," they said, "why are you weeping?"

"Because they have taken away my Lord," answered Mary, "and I do not know where they have laid him."

Mary then became aware of someone behind her. She turned around and saw a man standing there, but she did not recognize him through her tears.

"Woman," said the man, "why are you crying? Whom are you seeking?"

"Sir," said Mary, supposing the man to be the gardener, "if you have carried Jesus' body away, please tell me where you have laid him."

"Mary!" said the man.

The voice startled Mary, for she would have recognized it anywhere. She lifted her head with a jerk, wiped away her tears as well as she could, and looked intently into the man's eyes. "*Rabboni!* Master!" she exclaimed with surprise.

"Do not hold onto me," said Jesus, "for I have not yet ascended to the Father. Rather, go to my brethren and tell them, 'I am ascending to my Father and your Father, and to my God and your God.'"

Then Mary Magdalene went away to the disciples and said, "I have seen the Lord!" She told them that Jesus was alive, and explained the details of how she had seen him and what he had said to her. However, the disciples did not believe her.

Meanwhile, some of the guards informed the chief priests about what had happened. When the priests assembled with the elders and had taken counsel, they gave a large sum of money to the soldiers and told them to say that Jesus' disciples came at night and stole his body while the soldiers slept.

When the soldiers objected that they could lose their lives if they admitted to being asleep or to allowing one they were guarding to escape, the priests assured them, "We will make certain that no harm comes to you if you do as we have said. Furthermore, if the governor hears of it, we will satisfy him so that you will have nothing to worry about."

The soldiers therefore took the money and did as they were instructed.

The Road to Emmaus

Later on Sunday, a follower of Jesus named Cleopas invited Joseph of Arimathea to come to his home in Emmaus, which was about seven miles from Jerusalem. Since Joseph was ceremonially unclean for seven days and had no desire to stay around Jerusalem, he accepted the offer.

As they left Jerusalem by the Western Gate and proceeded along the road to Emmaus, Cleopas and Joseph discussed the events that had happened during the Passover, including the crucifixion of Jesus.

"I can't believe that he's dead," said Cleopas sadly. "I really thought he was the Messiah."

"So did I," admitted Joseph. "I even assigned several of my best investigators to follow Jesus and to find out his background. All the pieces seemed to fit … ."

"Yes. That's why we all welcomed him into Jerusalem as a conquering hero."

"What a difference one week makes."

"A week ago I eagerly anticipated his coming kingdom."

"From eager anticipation to dejected misery … in seven short days. Do you remember his triumphant entry into Jerusalem?" asked Joseph. "I really and truly thought the Passover would mark the beginning of the Messianic redemption of our nation. The days of Roman occupation were numbered; the Messiah's eternal reign was about to begin."

"Yes," said Cleopas. "Our future has been dark for so many centuries. All we had to look forward to was a promise God seemed to have forgotten. Then Jesus came and filled us with anticipation. Unfortunately, everything suddenly changed. He was put to death. Our future is dark again—and I'm left with an agonizing longing and an incredible aching empty feeling."

"Why's that?" asked a stranger who had joined them while Cleopas was talking.

"Oh! You startled me," said Cleopas. "We were just talking among ourselves."

"You seem to be awfully sad and dejected," observed the stranger.

"Well, of course we're dejected," snapped Cleopas. "After what has just happened in Jerusalem, why shouldn't we be sad?"

"What things are you referring to?"

Cleopas was dumbfounded. "You must be the only man in Jerusalem who has not heard about the things that have happened there these past few days!" he remarked.

"What things?" repeated the stranger.

"The things concerning Jesus of Nazareth," Cleopas answered. "Jesus was a prophet who was mighty in deed and word before God and all the people, but the chief priests and our religious rulers handed him over to be condemned to death, and he was crucified."

"We were hoping that he was the promised Messiah who would redeem Israel and establish his kingdom forever," added Joseph. "Unfortunately, we were obviously mistaken, since the Messiah cannot rule forever if he is dead—and this is now the third day since he died."

"Are you sure he's dead?" asked the stranger.

"Of course I'm sure," Joseph replied. "Not only did I watch him die, but I even helped take him down from the cross and buried him in my own tomb."

"Another thing that has added to our concern," Cleopas said, "is that some women of our company were at the tomb early this morning and did not find his body, and came back saying that they had seen a vision of angels claiming Jesus is alive. Then some of the disciples went to the tomb and found it just as the women had said, but they did not see either the body of Jesus or the angels."

"How foolish you are, and how slow of heart to believe all that the prophets have spoken!" the stranger exclaimed. "Wasn't it necessary for the Messiah to suffer these things before entering his glory?" And beginning with Moses and all the prophets, he explained to them the things that had been written about the Messiah in all the scriptures.

By this point, they had arrived at the village of Emmaus. Since it appeared that the stranger was preparing to continue down the road, Cleopas and Joseph begged him to remain, saying, "Stay here with us, for the evening is at hand and the day is far spent."

The three men went in to Cleopas' house and sat at the table together. The stranger took the bread, broke it, and prayed, "Our heavenly Father, may your name be honored and glorified. May your will be done on earth even as it is in heaven. Please meet our basic needs each day. Forgive our sins and trespasses against you, as we also forgive others' sins and trespasses against us. Bless this bread to the good of our bodies, and bless these men who are now entrusted with spreading your gospel message. Guide them and help them to know your truth and your way. May they have the courage to do what they know to be right, for yours is the kingdom and the power and the glory forever. Amen."

When he finished his prayer, the man looked at Joseph and Cleopas. Both men were staring in dumbfounded awe at him. After several moments, Joseph stammered, "Jesus ... it really *is* you, isn't it?"

Jesus merely smiled and said, "Peace be with you, Joseph. And also with you, Cleopas. *Shalom.*" At that moment he vanished from their sight.

"Wait!" shouted Cleopas. "Where'd he go, Joseph? How could he just disappear like that?"

"I don't know," Joseph answered as he franticly looked around the room.

"We weren't talking to a ghost, were we?"

"No," Joseph replied. "He appeared very solid and substantial. I also don't think ghosts can break bread the way he did."

"Then how did he just vanish?"

"His resurrected body must permit him to do that," answered Joseph. "But he at least confirmed what the women claimed—and he answered my questions."

"Yes," Cleopas agreed. "My heart burned within me as he spoke to us along the way and opened up the scriptures to us."

"Same here. But if that's the case, why are we still standing here blabbering about it? We should tell the other disciples the good news!"

They got up from the table at once and hurried back to Jerusalem. Although they felt compelled to tell Jesus' disciples about what they had seen and heard, Joseph insisted on first stopping at Nicodemus' house.

"Come with us ... now," Joseph urged Nicodemus. "We have something wonderful, important and exciting we must tell Jesus' disciples, but I want you to be present when we do so."

"Why?" Nicodemus asked.

"You know the scriptures better than we do. Although the meaning of the scriptures concerning the Messiah has been revealed to us, we need you present so that you can help us with the scriptural references. Also, what we have to tell the disciples directly concerns some of the things you and I have been discussing."

Seeing the depth of Joseph's excitement and how that contrasted with the deep despair he was feeling, Nicodemus consented. "All right, friend. I will come with you."

As they walked to the house where Jesus' disciples were staying, Joseph and Cleopas told how Jesus had appeared to them on the road to Emmaus. Nicodemus initially refused to believe that Jesus was alive.

"Joseph, you and I *buried* him. You remember how stiff he was and how hard it was to move and bathe his body, don't you?

"Absolutely—but Cleopas and I have seen him and talked with him just a little while ago. I *know* he has risen from the dead and that he now lives again!"

Nicodemus walked silently beside his two friends for several moments, his mind reeling as he thought of the implications. It was obvious to him that both Joseph and Cleopas were convinced that Jesus had risen from the dead and was alive again. As he turned these things over in his mind, Nicodemus began to chuckle.

"What's so funny?" asked Joseph.

"Do you remember when we met with Jesus that first night several years ago?"

"Of course."

"Do you remember how he startled me by announcing that we must be born again?"

"Yes."

"Who would have imagined that he would start with himself?"

Joseph stared blankly at his friend. Then he nodded twice and grinned. Both men laughed.

When they arrived at the house where Jesus' disciples were staying, they found only ten of the disciples there, cowering behind locked and barred doors. Judas had hanged himself, and the disciples had not been able to locate Thomas. Joseph and Cleopas told the others what had happened on the road to Emmaus, how they did not recognize Jesus until he broke bread with them, and how he had then vanished from their sight.

"Didn't I tell you?" Peter exclaimed to the other disciples.

"Peter has been telling us that Jesus appeared to him earlier today," Andrew said. "We refused to believe it when the women first told us this morning—but now I'm not so sure."

"I would like to believe he's alive," James said, "but I can't get past the fact that those Roman soldiers are professional killers who would not have allowed someone to survive a crucifixion."

"Oh, Jesus was dead," John said. "I personally saw his body go limp after he stopped fighting for breath, and I saw the Roman soldier thrust his spear through Jesus' side. But I also saw the empty tomb this morning. The linen was still wound around the place where Jesus' body had been—like an empty cocoon. As I said before, a grave robber would not take the body and leave the expensive spices and linen."

"Still, an empty tomb is not necessarily the same as a risen rabbi—though I desperately want him to be alive," Matthew said. "Being with Jesus these past three years has been the most remarkable period of my life."

The other disciples affirmed their agreement.

"I gave up a lucrative business to follow him, but I've never regretted it," Matthew continued. "All my life I've been interested in the word of God and how it might apply to me as a person. I have especially treasured the moments when Jesus explained the meanings of the scriptures to me … ."

"That's what he did for us on the road to Emmaus," Joseph interjected.

"Did he explain why God would allow his Messiah to die?" asked Matthew. "I had always believed the Messiah would reign forever."

"We also thought that," Joseph said, "but Jesus quoted numerous scriptures and explained why it had to be done."

"Tell me, please"

"There were more scriptures than I can remember," Joseph began, "but perhaps we can remember enough to give you the general ideas Jesus presented about the prophecies and their fulfillment.

"First, let me say that I—like so many other Jews—have been longing for a political or military Messiah. I prayed that God would send one who would deliver us from Roman rule, reestablish the glory Israel experienced under David and Solomon, and reign over that kingdom forever. So desperate were we that I forgot the Deliverer would be God's Messiah to the whole world rather than merely a Jewish Messiah imposing Jewish rule over the earth. My fixation on using my interpretation of a few scriptures may have caused me to overlook the many scriptures that showed us God's objective was to deliver his people from their sins, rather than merely posting another king to overthrow foreign rulers."

"But that is already being done," James objected. "Isn't that why we sacrifice lambs as guilt offerings in the temple?"

186

"Yes, you're right," Cleopas answered. "After man's relationship with God was severed by man's sin, God made it possible for our sins to be forgiven. God said he would take the blood of the lamb as a substitute for the sinner's blood."

"You see," Joseph added, "God made a covenant with us. If we would repent of our sins and sacrifice a lamb without spot or blemish, God would accept the blood of the lamb as a substitute for our blood and would forgive us of our sin."

"Notice that it is the sinner who deserves to die, James," Nicodemus interjected. "The lamb hadn't sinned or done anything wrong. It is God's mercy, grace, and forgiveness that saves us and counts us as being righteous."

"Then why would God send the Messiah to do what was already being done?" James asked.

"Jesus explained to us that throughout history, God has promised that when he thought the time was right, he would replace the old covenant with a new and better covenant that would rest on the Lord himself presenting the perfect Lamb of God to shed his blood—once and for all time—as a sacrifice for the remission of our sins," Joseph replied. "I had not realized it previously, but this was the true mission of the Messiah: to save his people from their sins."

"All of us have sinned and come short of the glory of God," Cleopas added. "Since no person is truly righteous, no human could serve as the perfect Lamb of God. Only God could live a life without sin and thus be the perfect sacrifice for our sins."

"But how could God—who is eternal, without either beginning or end—possibly die?" asked John.

"Ah, now you sound like my friend Nicodemus, here," Joseph smiled. Turning to Nicodemus, he said, "Do you remember our conversation after Mary revealed that the angel Gabriel had told her that God would use a part of his own pure energy or spirit to impregnate her, so that the holy one to be born from her womb would be called the Son of God? You then said that the resulting child would be part of the same God—except that now that part of God would exist in human form and with certain human restrictions. You also said you had no idea why God would do such a thing."

"I remember," Nicodemus admitted.

"Jesus explained that part to us. Only God could be the perfect sacrifice, for only God can live without sinning. However, since Almighty God is eternal and cannot die, it became necessary for him to use a part of his divine Spirit to form a human version of himself that was bound by human restrictions and subject to the dimensions that restrict the rest of us."

"You mean, uh…" stammered Nicodemus. "Do you mean to say that God actually took on human limitations in order to sacrifice himself as a payment for the sins *we* have committed?"

"That's precisely what I mean to say," Joseph answered, "because that is what the resurrected Jesus told us."

"That's incredible!" Nicodemus marveled. "That's unbelievable. That's a love I can hardly fathom…"

"Yes, but that was God's plan all along," Joseph said. "That's why the Christ child could be born into this world, could live a life without sin—thus becoming the perfect Lamb of God, could teach and instruct us while living, and then could freely offer himself as the perfect sacrifice for our sins."

"That's right," Cleopas exclaimed. "Jesus pointed out that his death and burial were abundantly foretold by Isaiah, Zechariah, and the Psalms, which all say that he would be rejected by his people,[63]

---

[63] Ps. 22:6; Isa. 53:3, 8.

would be struck and beaten,[64] would remain silent in the face of false accusations,[65] would be scorned and mocked,[66] would be led like a lamb to the slaughter,[67] would be smitten, afflicted and pierced,[68] and would thirst[69] and be offered vinegar.[70] I left out some of the prophesies Jesus mentioned. Joseph, help me."

"Those prophesies also said that people would divide his garments among themselves,[71] would cast lots for his clothing,[72] and would pierce his hands and feet,[73] but would not break any of his bones,[74]" Joseph said. "People would hurl insults at him, saying that since he trusts in God, let the Lord rescue him.[75]"

"Wait!" Peter objected. "Are you sure the prophets said all that?"

"Oh, they said it, all right," Nicodemus interjected. "But I hadn't really made the connection to how those scriptures applied to the Messiah."

"What about the prophesies of the all-conquering king who would reign forever?" Peter asked.

"Jesus told us that part comes later," Cleopas answered.

"When?"

"He didn't say."

"He said his current mission was to save his people from their sins and to institute God's new covenant with mankind," Joseph said.

---

[64] Isa. 52:14; 53:5, 7-8.
[65] Isa. 53:7.
[66] Ps. 22:7, 17; 69: 19-20; Isa. 50:6.
[67] Isa. 53:7, 10.
[68] Ps. 22:16; Isa. 53:4-5, 7; Zech. 12:10.
[69] Ps. 22:15.
[70] Ps. 69:21.
[71] Ps. 22:18.
[72] Ps. 22:18.
[73] Ps. 22:16.
[74] Ps. 34:20.
[75] Ps. 22:7-8.

"Yes, that's right," Cleopas added. "Because it was the Lord's will to crush him and cause him to suffer as a guilt offering, Isaiah said he would be stricken for the transgressions of his people, and he would be buried in a rich man's grave."[76]

"That's where you and I came in," Joseph grinned at Nicodemus.

Nicodemus smiled and nodded.

Cleopas continued, "The prophesies say he would not be abandoned in the grave, nor would God allow his body to decay.[77] The purpose for all of this is also given—to serve as a guilt offering for our sins so that we might be redeemed and have peace."[78]

"There are numerous other prophesies as well," Joseph interjected. "For example, we have often talked about the prophesies of Isaiah, Jeremiah, Ezekiel, and Psalms that he would be a descendant of David, and those of Isaiah and Micah that he would be born of a virgin in the town of Bethlehem."

"Yes," Nicodemus agreed. "We have gone over those at length the past few years. And we have also talked about how Isaiah said that the Messiah would be preceded by a forerunner to prepare the way, that he would have a Galilean ministry, and he would heal the blind and the lame. Zechariah talks about his triumphant entry into Jerusalem riding on a donkey. I quoted that one to you when he came into the city, if you remember."

"That you did, my friend," Joseph replied.

"The Psalms say he would be betrayed by a close trusted friend with whom he had shared bread,[79]" Nicodemus continued. "Zechariah revealed that the traitor would receive thirty pieces of

---

[76] Isa. 53:9-12.
[77] Ps. 16:10.
[78] Isa. 53:5-6, 10-12.
[79] Ps. 41:9.

silver, which would then be thrown back to the temple officials so that they could purchase a field from the pottery makers.[80] Amos prophesized that the Lord would darken the earth at midday."[81]

"Yes," said John, "I think it is becoming clearer to me now. In the beginning was the Word, and the Word was with God, and the Word was God—and the Word became flesh and dwelt among us ... because God loves us enough to make it possible for us to have everlasting life."

"Of course!" Nicodemus exclaimed, snapping his fingers. "That must be what Jesus meant when he said that part about Moses lifting up the serpent in the wilderness. You remember, don't you, John?"

"I'm not sure," John responded. "Remind me, if you will."

"That night when Jesus met with us, he said that just as Moses lifted up the snake in the desert, so must the Son of Man be lifted up, that everyone who believes in him might have eternal life. Jesus was lifted up on the cross to be our savior and our redeemer. If we believe in him, then he becomes our perfect sacrifice before God so that our sins may be covered over and forgiven, and we can have eternal life with God in heaven."

Turning toward Joseph, Nicodemus gestured with his hands as he continued, "That also would be the reason why the veil of the temple was ripped apart when he died. The old covenant requiring thousands of imperfect lambs to be slain is finished. God has instituted the new covenant where Jesus is the perfect Lamb of God."

"Excuse me," said Peter, "but I don't understand what you are talking about."

---

[80] Zech. 11:12-13.
[81] Amos 8:9.

"Well, Peter," began Nicodemus, "the curtain I am talking about is the extremely thick and strong inner veil that separates the Holy Place from the Holy of Holies. At the time Jesus died on the cross, an earthquake rocked Jerusalem. I was told by some of the priests who were in the Holy Place at the time of the earthquake that as they watched, the great inner veil of the temple was supernaturally ripped from top to bottom, causing the Holy of Holies to be exposed to their view."

"Why would God do that?" Peter asked.

"Great question!" Nicodemus exclaimed as he jumped up and began pacing back and forth—as he often did when excited or agitated. "Why *would* God open up the Holy of Holies by ripping apart the temple's inner veil?"

Nicodemus looked from one disciple to another as if he expected a response, but none of them attempted to answer the question.

"Don't you see?" he continued. "God made an emphatic statement that Christ's atoning sacrifice of dying for our sins made all other sin sacrifices pointless. The curtain no longer had any meaning, since God has opened the way to the Holy of Holies for all who are willing to confess their sins, accept Christ as their savior, and accept God's new covenant with mankind. Jesus' parents were instructed by the angel to call his name Jesus *because he would save his people from their sins.* The torn veil was God's way of saying that Jesus' mission had been successfully accomplished."

"Are you saying that God is no longer requiring us to sacrifice lambs as a guilt offering for our sins?" asked Peter.

"That's precisely what I'm saying," Nicodemus replied. "Although we may try to offer a lamb without a physical spot or blemish, it is still an imperfect sacrifice spiritually."

"What do you mean?"

"The lamb was not tempted to sin the same way we have been tempted. Christ, on the other hand, was tempted in all ways—yet he did not yield to those temptations. By living a sinless life, he became the perfect sacrifice for our sins. As John the Baptist said, Jesus was the Lamb of God who takes away the sins of the world."

"How can you be so sure that the old sacrifices are no longer needed?" Peter asked.

"Because God ripped the curtain covering the Holy of Holies! Perhaps an even more important reason is the fact that God resurrected Jesus from the grave," Nicodemus answered. "That means that God's holy curse against sin has been fully absorbed. The resurrection proves that God is satisfied that the price of forgiveness was paid in full by Jesus' death."

Nicodemus grasped Joseph by the shoulders and exclaimed, "Do you remember our discussion about how unsatisfying was the legalism of the old covenant?"

"I think so," Joseph nodded.

"Well, God's Messiah has ushered in the new and better covenant prophesied by Jeremiah."

As the disciples murmured among themselves at Nicodemus's words, Jesus himself suddenly appeared in their midst and said, "Peace be to you."

The disciples shrank back away from him. "It's his ghost!" declared James.

"Why are you troubled?" asked Jesus.

"Why?" sputtered Peter. "You suddenly materialize in a room where the doors are bolted—and then ask why we are troubled?

"Why do doubts arise in your minds and hearts?" asked Jesus, gently shaking his head and smiling. "Here—you may examine my hands and feet. Touch me and see for yourselves that it is I myself, for a spirit does not have flesh and bones as you see that I have." As Jesus said this, he showed them his hands and feet. As the disciples continued to stand in awe-struck wonder, Jesus asked them, "Do you have anything here that I could eat?" They gave him a piece of broiled fish, and he took it and ate as they watched.[82]

Then Jesus said to them, "These are the things I told you while I was still with you, that all the things written about me in the Law of Moses and in the prophets and psalms must be fulfilled." Jesus thus admitted to them again that he was indeed the Messiah.

He then opened their minds so that they might understand the scriptures, saying to them, "Thus it is written, that the Messiah should suffer and on the third day rise from the dead, that repentance and forgiveness of sins should be preached in his name to all nations, beginning at Jerusalem. You are witnesses of these things. I will send the promised Spirit of my Father upon you, but tarry in the city of Jerusalem until you are clothed with power from above."

Jesus turned to Joseph and Nicodemus, laid his hands on their shoulders, and said, "I told you earlier that you were not far from the kingdom of God. Do each of you now believe?"

"Yes, Lord," they both replied. "We now believe."

"You have sought the way of the Lord and diligently tried to learn the truth. I tell you now that I am the way, the truth and the life. I

---

[82] Thus, Jesus showed that he really was alive again and that his resurrected body had certain familiar characteristics: He could see and communicate, and could speak and be understood; he looked sufficiently similar to his prior self to be generally recognized; his wounds were visible and material; he had flesh and bones, was substantial, and could be touched; and he consumed food as a living, physical mortal body would. However, there were also some differences about his resurrected body, since he could transport himself through walls or doors.

have springs of living water available to those who thirst after righteousness. The Prince of Peace offers those who believe in him a peace that surpasses all understanding. May the peace of God abide in all of you, as you abide in me."

With that, Jesus vanished from their sight.

When the disciples found Thomas the next day, they told him that Jesus really was alive again and that he had appeared to them. Thomas exclaimed, "I don't believe you. You've been through so much these past few days that you must have been imagining things. I watched him die and saw that Roman soldier thrust a spear through the Master's side. I watched his body being taken from the cross and placed in the tomb. No! In order for me to believe what you now say, I would have to see the Lord for myself. Unless I can see in his hands the print of the nails, can put my finger on the scars left by those nails, and can put my hand into the place where the spear was thrust through his side, I will not believe!"

The following Sunday Thomas got his proof. Once again the disciples were gathered together, but this time Thomas was with them. Suddenly Jesus was also in the room. He looked directly at Thomas, smiled at him, and said, "Look at my hands and feet, feel my scars with your fingers, and put your hand into my side. Most of all, stop doubting and have faith."

Thomas reverently sank to his knees and exclaimed, "My Lord and my God!"

Simon Peter witnessed the redemption of Thomas and longed for similar catharsis. Although he did not doubt that Jesus had been resurrected and was alive, he did doubt that he could ever be forgiven for the three times he had denied his Lord.

Whenever Peter was deeply troubled, he found solace in his boat and nets. "I'm going fishing," he announced to the other disciples.

Six of his friends went with him. Although several of them were professional fishermen, they caught nothing after working hard all night long. Discouraged and disgruntled, they silently rowed back toward shore in the early predawn light the next morning.

Someone on the shore had a campfire burning. The stranger called out to them, "Friends, have you caught anything?"

"No," Peter yelled back.

"Let your net down on the right side of your ship, and you will catch some fish."

"That's crazy," grumbled Peter. "The only difference that would make is that it is harder to put out the nets on that side, since our boat is designed for casting the nets from the left."

"Well, we can't do any worse than what we've done so far," remarked John.

"Right you are, lad," Peter said as he joined the others in casting the net from the starboard side of the boat. The net was immediately filled with so many fish that they could not haul it in.

Remembering a similar event three years earlier when Jesus had initially called them to be his disciples, John whirled around and squinted into the pale light of morning. "It is the Lord!" he announced.

That was enough for Simon Peter, who immediately put on his clothes and jumped overboard and swam to shore, leaving the others to maneuver the boat back by themselves.

As they sat around the fire cooking some of the fish they had caught, Jesus turned to Peter and asked, "Simon, son of Jonas, do you love me more than these?"

Peter hesitated. He wasn't sure whether Jesus was asking whether he loved him more than did the other disciples or if he loved Jesus more than his former life of being a fisherman—but either way he could answer, "Yes, Lord, you know that I love you."

"Then feed my lambs," Jesus said.

John mentally noted that when Jesus had asked the question, he used the Greek word *agape*—but Peter answered with the Greek word *philia*. Thus, the Lord had asked, "Simon, son of Jonas, do you unconditionally love me more than these?" Peter had answered, "Yes, Lord, you know that I love you as a brother."

Jesus asked the disciple a second time, "Simon, son of Jonas, do you unconditionally love me?"

Again Peter answered, "Yes, Lord, you know I love you like a brother."

"Then take care of my sheep."

The third time Jesus asked the question, he used *philia* instead of *agape*—in effect asking, "Simon, son of Jonas, do you even love me as a brother?"

Although Peter was hurt by the question, he responded, "Lord, you know everything. You know I love you."

"Feed my sheep."

Three times had Simon Peter denied even knowing his Lord. Three times he had been asked to pledge his love, and three times he was given an assignment to shepherd the Master's flock. Peter had been forgiven and reinstated as a leader of the disciples. From that moment on, he was truly a fisher of men as he preached the gospel of his crucified and risen Lord.

Jesus later gathered his disciples together and told them, "I have been given all authority in heaven and on earth. As you go into all the world, preach the gospel to the people of all nations, and make them my disciples. Baptize them in the name of the Father, the Son, and the Holy Spirit, and teach them to do everything I have told you. I will be with you always—even to the end of the world."

Jesus appeared to hundreds of people over the forty days following his death, burial, and resurrection. The final such appearance was on the eastern slope of the Mount of Olives near Bethany, where he taught them and blessed them before ascending into heaven. As the disciples and other followers continued looking into the skies, two angels in dazzling white appeared and asked, "Why are you standing here looking into the sky? Jesus has been taken to heaven. Go back into Jerusalem and wait until you have been empowered by God's Holy Spirit."

Pentecost

Ten days later, the disciples gathered in the same upper room they had used for their final celebration of Passover with Jesus. The delectably tangy smell of freshly baked loaves of leavened bread wafted up from the kitchen. The loaves were made from recently harvested grain for Pentecost, which was observed fifty days after Passover. A couple of the disciples were preparing the table and couches for the Pentecost meal while others in the group lounged near the table and engaged each other in quiet conversation.

Their reverie was shattered by the sound of a mighty wind approaching.

"Storm's coming," yelled Peter as he ducked between two couches.

John sprinted for the doorway to the stairs.

Others frantically looked around for some place to hide or at least for something to give them shelter.

Suddenly the house filled with brilliant radiant light so bright the disciples had to shield their eyes. Visible within the radiant glow were myriads of small flickering flames.

"Fire!" bellowed Peter as he bolted for the door. Phillip and Bartholomew both ran toward the doorway. They collided, and Bartholomew fell down. As he got up, Bartholomew grabbed the basin of water the disciples had used for washing their feet and sloshed the water at James' head.

"What the...?" exclaimed James indignantly.

"Sorry," Bartholomew mumbled. "I was just trying to save you from that fire." He pointed toward James' head, which was surrounded by flickering flames which were apparently unaffected by the water.

"You've got one too," said James as they clambered down the stairs. The light of the morning sun was not as bright as the brilliant light inside the upper room. The disciples, who had all fled the upper room, looked at one another in wonder and confusion. They saw what appeared to be flaming bits of fire settling on each of them. The fire then merged with each of the disciples, and their faces glowed with radiant light.

"What's happening to us?" asked Bartholomew.

"I have no idea," James answered, "but I feel strangely euphoric."

"I do, too," said John. "Whatever it is, the glow each of us has looks somewhat similar to the glow Jesus had when he was transfigured on top of that mountain."

"You're right," James exclaimed, "though his may have been somewhat stronger."

"Could this be the comforter or counselor Jesus said he would be sending?" John asked.

"The what?"

"Don't you remember? Jesus said we were to wait in Jerusalem until God sent us his Holy Spirit. Maybe that's what this is."

"What is this Holy Spirit of which you speak?" asked a stranger.

The disciples looked around to discover that hundreds of people had converged upon them. Thousands of others were following, apparently drawn by the unusual sound of the approaching wind. The strangers were raptly listening to everything the disciples said.

"Ptolemy!" exclaimed another stranger to the first man. "How is it that you can understand what these men are saying?

"Why wouldn't I?"

"Because they are conversing in Latin." Turning to John, the second stranger explained, "Since Ptolemy only speaks Egyptian, I have to translate everything for him."

"What language are you speaking?" asked John.

"Latin, of course—the same as you."

"I thought I was speaking Aramaic—but I fully understand everything both of you are saying."

"Excuse me, another stranger said to John. "Are you claiming that you are speaking Aramaic?"

"Yes," said John.

"I also speak Aramaic—but I am hearing you in my native Parthian tongue."

"What do you mean?" asked John.

"I am a native Parthian, and all of you seem to be speaking my language fluently."

"I am hearing—and understanding—all of you in Egyptian," said Ptolemy as he put a hand on the second stranger's shoulder. "It's wonderful to not have to depend upon Marcus to translate everything for me."

"How is this possible?" asked Marcus. "I hear you speaking in Latin, while Ptolemy hears you speaking in Egyptian, and Seneca hears you speaking Parthian."

Parthians, Medes, Elamites, Mesopotamians, Greeks, Judeans, Cappadocians, Egyptians, Libyans, Romans, Asians and various other people—both native Jews and converts to Judaism—were present in Jerusalem for Pentecost. Amazed yet perplexed that they each could understand the gospel message in their native tongues, several questioned what was happening. One of them asked, "What does this mean?"

"We have been filled with the Spirit of the living God," John answered.

"Filled with spirits is more like it," one of the strangers laughed. "I think they're drunk. Maybe that's why their faces have that strange glow."

Then Peter addressed the crowd, "These men are not drunk; people don't generally get drunk by nine o'clock in the morning—and liquor doesn't cause people's faces to radiate light. Rather, this is fulfillment of what the prophet Joel prophesied when he said:

In the last days, God says,
I will pour out my Spirit on all people.
Your sons and daughters will prophesy,
Your young men will see visions;
your old men will dream dreams.
Even on my servants, both men and women,
I will pour out my Spirit in those days, and they will prophesy.
I will show wonders in the heaven above
and signs on the earth below.
And everyone who calls on the name of the Lord
will be saved.[83]

"Men of Israel, listen to this: Jesus of Nazareth was a man accredited by God to you by miracles, wonders, and signs, which God did among you through him, as you yourselves know. This man was handed over to you by God's set purpose and foreknowledge, and you with the help of wicked men put him to death by nailing him to the cross. But God raised him from the dead, freeing him from the agony of death."

---

[83] Joel 2:28-32.

Peter looked over the crowd. All the men and women were listening intently to what he had to say. It was obvious to him that all of them could clearly understand him even though they spoke various languages. God's Spirit was at work in a mighty way.

"David also prophesied of this when he spoke of the resurrection of the Messiah and said that he would not be abandoned to the grave, nor would his body decay. God has raised Jesus to life, and we are all witnesses of that fact." Peter motioned to the other disciples, and they in turn affirmed that it was true. Peter concluded, "Therefore let all Israel be assured of this: God has made this Jesus, whom you crucified, both Lord and Messiah. The fact that all of you can understand me in your native language is proof that God's Holy Spirit is working a mighty miracle here today."

Someone in the crowd called out, "Brothers, what shall we do?"

Peter replied, "Repent and be baptized, every one of you, in the name of Jesus Christ for the forgiveness of your sins. Then you will also receive God's gift of his Holy Spirit."

Peter and the other disciples met with the crowd of onlookers and answered their questions. Those who accepted the gospel message were baptized, and about three thousand persons were added to the number of believers that day.

*****

Across town, Joseph of Arimathea and one of his stewards were inventorying the goods being carried by one of his caravans when the steward suddenly gave a cry of alarm and jumped back away from Joseph.

"What's wrong with you?" asked Joseph.

"You're on fire!" exclaimed the man.

"What?" cried Joseph as he quickly examined his garments, but saw no sign of a fire.

"No. It's on your head!" said the steward.

Joseph felt of his head, but found no fire. He did, however, feel suddenly different. An energy he had never felt before seemed to consume him. Since he wasn't sure what to say or do, Joseph merely looked questioningly at the steward.

"It's gone now," said the steward, "but your face has a strange glow about it."

"I think I may need to check on something," Joseph remarked. "Go ahead and finish the inventory on your own, and I'll meet with you again tomorrow morning."

The steward merely nodded his head. He was not sure he wanted to be around someone who seemed to have fire flickering around his head. *It might be time to look for another job,* he thought.

Joseph hurried to the home of Nicodemus and beat on the door until a servant opened it.

"Is Nicodemus home?" Joseph asked.

"Yes. He's in the courtyard garden."

"I must see him immediately," Joseph said as he pushed past the servant. He walked briskly to the courtyard, where he saw Nicodemus talking excitedly with other members of his household.

"Nicodemus," Joseph called as he burst into the courtyard, "I must talk to you immediately about … "

"About the Holy Spirit descending and filling us?" Nicodemus interrupted. "Yes, we were just discussing that. I see from your radiance that you have also been filled."

"What … what are you talking about?" Joseph stammered.

"That is why you are here, isn't it?" asked Nicodemus. "Didn't you also have what appeared to be flickering tongues of fire land on you and then fill you with the Spirit of God?"

"I don't know. I didn't see it, but that agrees with what my steward said he saw. Well, actually, he said I was on fire."

"Yes—on fire for the Lord," Nicodemus smiled. "Luckily, all of us here are believers. Thus, when the Holy Spirit came, we could all see it on one another. Didn't your investigator report that John the Baptist said that God's Holy Spirit would baptize believers with fire?"

"Hmmmm. What was it that he said?" Joseph mulled. "I'm thinking that John said he baptized with water, but the one coming soon would baptize with God's Holy Spirit and with fire. I thought he meant that the Messiah would do those things."

"Either way, it appears to me that this may be what he was talking about. I suggest that we pay a visit to Jesus' disciples. I wouldn't be surprised if their experience was truly remarkable."

When Nicodemus and Joseph got near the upper room, they saw that a huge number of people had gathered. Peter had finished his message to the crowd, and the disciples were visiting with all who had questions. Nicodemus and Joseph joined in the discussions and also gave testimony to what they knew and believed.

"It was incredible!" John told them. "The room was filled with such brightness that we were compelled to come outside."

"Was it just a bright light, or was there something else?" Nicodemus asked.

"Something else," John responded. "The light had an awesomely glorious aura about it that I can't explain. It totally filled the room—and it now seems to be filling us as well."

"Yes, that pretty well describes God's shekhinah glory," Nicodemus said.

"Shekhi ... what?"

"Shekhinah. That's what we call the awesome radiance of God's glory. When the tabernacle was first constructed and dedicated, God

205

showed his approval by filling the tent with his shekhinah glory to such an extent that Moses was unable to enter the tabernacle. Now God has apparently chosen to fill us with his spirit. As John the Baptist prophesized, we have been baptized with God's Holy Spirit and with fire."

*****

Being filled with God's Holy Spirit made a dramatic difference in the believers' lives and actions. They no longer cowered behind locked doors. Instead, they boldly proclaimed the good news of God's new covenant to all they met—even in the temple.

One afternoon, Peter and John were entering the Beautiful Gate of the temple when a man who had been crippled from birth called out to them, hoping they would give him some money. Looking intently at the crippled beggar, Peter said, "I do not have any silver or gold, but what I do have I will give to you. In the name of Jesus Christ of Nazareth, stand up and walk."

Peter then reached out, took the beggar by the right hand, and helped him stand up on his feet. The man's feet and ankles immediately became strong, and he started walking—gingerly at first, but soon he was leaping and jumping around. He even picked up the mat upon which he had been lying and danced a jig with it. As Peter and John continued on into the temple courts, the beggar walked with them, praising and glorifying God.

Since many people recognized the beggar as being the man who had been crippled from birth who had to be carried by friends to the Beautiful Gate each day to beg, a sizeable crowd soon gathered around the three men. Peter turned to the people and said, "Men of Israel, why does this surprise you? Why do you stare at us as if we made this man walk by our own power?

"The God of our fathers—Abraham, Isaac, and Jacob—has glorified his servant Jesus. You handed him over to be killed by the Romans; you disowned him before Pilate and asked that a murderer be released to you. You killed the author of life, but God raised him from the dead. We are witnesses of this."

Many in the crowd murmured among themselves, but they still listened intently to Peter.

"By faith in the name of Jesus, this man whom you see and know was made strong," Peter continued. "It is Jesus' name and the faith that comes through him that has given this complete healing to him, as you all can see." The crowd looked intently at the beggar, who nodded affirmatively that what Peter said was true.

"Now, brothers," Peter continued, "I know that you acted in ignorance, as did your leaders. But this is how God fulfilled what he had foretold through all the prophets, saying that his Messiah would suffer. Moses and all the prophets from Samuel on have foretold these days. And you are heirs of the prophets and of the covenant God made with your fathers. He said to Abraham, 'Through your offspring—the Messiah—all the peoples of the earth will be blessed.' God raised Jesus from the dead and has sent us to proclaim the good news so that you may turn from your wicked ways and have an everlasting relationship with God."

A burly captain of the temple guard pushed his way through the crowd surrounding Peter and John. A sword was strapped to his left side, and he brandished a whip in his right hand. Following in his wake were Caiaphas, Annas, and Matthias. The captain strode up to Peter and John while they were speaking to the people, paused, and looked back to Caiaphas. The high priest nodded to the captain and gestured with both hands toward the two disciples. The captain seized both men and put them into the temple jail.

The next day, Peter and John were brought before an assembly of rulers, elders, and teachers of Jewish law. The high priest, Caiaphas, demanded, "By what power did you heal the crippled beggar?"

Peter answered, "Rulers and elders of the people, if we are being called to account today for an act of kindness shown to a cripple and are asked how he was healed, then you should know that it is by the name of Jesus Christ of Nazareth, whom you crucified but whom God raised from the dead, that this man stands before you healed."

Angry mutters erupted from several members of the Sanhedrin.

"Jesus is 'the stone you builders rejected, which has now become the capstone.'" Peter continued above a rising tide of dissent. "Salvation is found in no one else, for there is no other name under heaven given to men by which we may be saved."

Caiaphas turned to the captain of the guard and said, "Take these men back to their cell while we deliberate among ourselves."

"How is it that these men dare to credit that imposter's name with such power?" asked Matthias. "He was condemned by this assembly for blasphemy and put to death."

"Aren't these the same men who scattered and ran when Jesus was arrested?" interjected Annas. "How is it that they now speak with such courage and determination?"

"What I would like to know," said a Pharisee named Gamaliel, "is how can unschooled, ordinary men such as these know scripture and prophesy as well as they do?"

"They may have been ordinary unschooled fishermen," noted Nicodemus, "but they also spent three years with Jesus as his disciples—and Jesus was very knowledgeable in scriptures and was a great teacher and rabbi."

Matthias turned to Caiaphas and said, "Didn't I warn you that Nicodemus had sold out to that charlatan Jesus and had become one of his followers?"

"Yes," muttered Caiaphas softly, "you did … ."

"We may have some disagreements regarding Jesus," Gamaliel said, "but there is no denying that a man who has been crippled from birth—crippled for over forty years, in fact—is now suddenly able to walk again. This miracle has been witnessed by over a thousand people. What are we going to do with these men? Everybody living in Jerusalem knows that they have done an outstanding miracle, and we cannot deny it."

"We must stop this from spreading any further," said Matthias.

"How?" asked Gamaliel.

"We will sternly warn these men not to use the name of Jesus in the future," answered Caiaphas. He then ordered Peter and John to be brought before the counsel.

"We have decided to let you go this time," Caiaphas announced, "but you are commanded not to speak or teach at all in the name of Jesus."

Peter responded, "Judge for yourselves whether it is right in God's sight to obey you rather than God."

John added, "God's Spirit compels us to obey his commands—and he compels us to speak truly, honestly and boldly about what we have seen and heard."

"Just remember what we did to your leader," Caiaphas sneered. "We have the power to do the same to you." He turned to the captain of the guard and ordered, "Release them."

As the Sanhedrin dispersed, Nicodemus walked over to Gamaliel and said softly, "May I have a few words with you in private?"

Gamaliel nodded his head, and the two men walked toward a quiet corner of the Portico of Solomon.

"These men have indeed been with Jesus," Nicodemus said. "Not just with the Jesus who taught and ministered among us for three years, but also with the resurrected Jesus. Being with one whom God has raised from the dead has emboldened and energized them to an extent you cannot imagine.

"They will not be silent," Nicodemus continued. "Indeed, they cannot be silent, for God's Holy Spirit compels them to do his will and carry out his commands. What concerns me is that the Sanhedrin may be working *against* God and his will."

"Nicodemus," said Gamaliel, "you and I are considered the principal teachers of Israel. We are the foremost authorities on the scriptures, the law and the prophets. As such, I have always had the highest regard for your opinions. Although neither of us was present when the Sanhedrin found Jesus guilty of blasphemy, the basic quorum of members still rendered judgment."

When Nicodemus started to object, Gamaliel quieted the objection by raising his hand and continuing, "Granted, we both question the legality of that proceeding. Nevertheless, the Sanhedrin rendered judgment, and Jesus was turned over to the Romans and executed."

Nicodemus nodded his head.

Gamaliel continued, "You reportedly then assisted another member of the Sanhedrin in giving Jesus a proper burial, even though you undoubtedly knew that action would not be viewed with favor by our high priest and a large segment of the Sanhedrin. Although some of our colleagues on the counsel think that was a rash action on your part, I think I know you well enough to know that you never do anything rashly. You must have examined the scriptures first and concluded that Jesus was either the Messiah or was someone else sent by God. Am I correct?"

"Yes, you are essentially correct," Nicodemus answered, and he summarized the evidence for Gamaliel.

"I can see why you have acted as you have," Gamaliel concluded, "and I also understand why you are concerned about the direction the Sanhedrin appears to be headed."

"Because of my actions on behalf of Jesus, many of those on the Sanhedrin will no longer listen to what I have to say," Nicodemus said.

"What do you want from me?"

"I ask that you prayerfully consider what I have said. If you agree that my words have merit, please do what you can to keep the Sanhedrin from opposing the will of God."

"That's a fair request," answered Gamaliel. "All right, my friend, I will prayerfully consider your words and your request. Shalom."

"Shalom."

Gamaliel

The apostles continued preaching the good news of Jesus and performed many miraculous signs and wonders among the people. Just as masses of people had once crowded around Jesus to be blessed by his healing powers, so now people brought the sick to the disciples so they might be cured.

So many people flocked to the temple in Jerusalem to see Peter and the other apostles that the high priest and Sadducees were consumed with jealousy. Once again they ordered the temple guards to arrest Jesus' disciples—but this time they did not stop with Peter and John.

Seven guards armed with swords and whips accompanied their captain as they pushed through the crowd, surrounded the apostles, placed them under arrest, and led them to the temple prison.

"What do you think they are going to do to us?" Thomas asked fearfully.

"I'm sure they'll punish us in some manner," John replied. "After all, they did command Peter and me to stop preaching and healing in Jesus' name."

"They crucified our master," Peter added.

"It's too late for them to assemble the Sanhedrin today," Bartholomew observed. "We'll probably find out our fate tomorrow."

Midnight came and went. One by one the disciples dropped off to sleep, as not even the cramped conditions, uncomfortable leg irons and hard floor could keep them awake indefinitely. In the early morning hours, they had an unexpected visitor.

"Wake up, all of you," the visitor urged softly as he shook them.

"Wha?—Who are you?" asked Peter.

"No time for that now," responded the visitor. "Follow me—but quietly."

As the disciples rose to their feet, the leg irons that had securely bound them fell off their ankles. The stranger held the door to their cell block open until all had passed through. When he shut it behind them, the distinctive click of the lock could be heard.

The visitor led the disciples past temple guards who continued to stand at their posts. The guards did not seem to see or hear them. When they arrived at another cell, the door opened as they approached. After they passed, that door also locked behind them.

When they were safely outside the temple, Peter asked the stranger, "Are you an angel?"

The stranger merely smiled and answered, "When the morning crowds come to the temple, you should go stand in the temple courts and tell the people the full message of this new life with God."

"Wait!" Peter insisted. "I thought angels had wings."

"Wings do not have to always be visible. In this case, stealth was more important than appearances. What is important is that you continue to carry out God's mission of telling the good news of the new covenant. This quiet rescue will help make the Jewish authorities hesitant to use excessive force at this time, but the time is approaching when you will be scattered." He then turned and disappeared from their sight.

At daybreak the apostles entered the temple courts and continued teaching the people and telling them the good news of the gospel.

Caiaphas called a special meeting of the Sanhedrin so that the disciples could be tried. When the Sanhedrin assembled, he sent word to the jail to bring the apostles before the court. When the officers went to the cells where the disciples had been imprisoned, they found the jail securely locked and all the guards properly on duty—but the apostles were no longer inside. The captain of the guard was at a loss as to what had happened.

One of the other temple guards then reported, "Sir, the men you put in jail are standing in the temple courts teaching the people."

The captain and a contingent of his guards followed the officer who had made the report, discovered the apostles teaching and healing in the temple courts just as the officer had reported, and brought them back to the Sanhedrin.

"We gave you strict orders not to teach or heal in the name of Jesus," Caiaphas said, "yet here you have filled Jerusalem with your teaching in direct violation of our order. You apparently intend to bring this man's blood upon us."

"We must obey God rather than men," answered Peter, speaking for the group.

"Do you know to whom you are speaking?" asked Caiaphas incredulously. "This," and he gestured to the assembled counsel, "is the Great Sanhedrin of Israel, the lawful body that has been duly commissioned to uphold the rule of God Almighty. How dare you imply that what is said or commanded by the Sanhedrin is not of God!"

"Yes, I know who you are," Peter replied. "You are the ones who had Jesus killed by hanging him on a cross. But the God of our fathers raised Jesus from the dead and then exalted him to his own right hand as Prince and Savior, that he might give repentance and forgiveness of sins. We are witnesses of these things, and so is the Holy Spirit, whom God has given to those who obey him."

Matthias jumped to his feet and exclaimed, "This is an outrage! Not only is this man speaking of a condemned criminal as if he were a prophet of God Almighty, but he is also asserting that this great assembly lacks God's Holy Spirit, while claiming that the group of ruffians who followed the condemned criminal known as Jesus has been granted special access to God."

Matthias' words met with favor from most of the Sanhedrin, who were clearly upset with what Peter had said. However, Gamaliel rose to his feet and held up both hands in a motion intended to quiet the assembly. When the noise level dropped enough for him to speak in a normal voice, Gamaliel said, "I suggest that the captain of the guard lead the prisoners outside so that I may have a word with the counsel."

Caiaphas nodded to the captain, who then took the apostles out of the room. All the members of the Sanhedrin then turned to listen to Gamaliel, who was the most honored sage and teacher among them.

"Men of Israel," cautioned Gamaliel, "take care what you do with these men."

"But we can't allow them to claim they are being led by God!" objected Matthias.

"Are you really and truly certain that God is *not* leading them?"

"We, the chief priests and the Great Sanhedrin, are the ones who have been duly appointed to speak for God—not these ruffians," Matthias said.

215

"Ah," nodded Gamaliel. "There's the real issue. Some of us are afraid that our own power and authority might be undermined."

Although Matthias recoiled at Gamaliel's comment, several other members of the Sanhedrin chuckled.

"Listen carefully to my counsel," Gamaliel cautioned. "Some time ago Theudas appeared and claimed to be a great leader. About four hundred men rallied to his cause—but when he was killed, all his followers dispersed, and it all came to nothing."

Murmurs of agreement indicated that members of the Sanhedrin remembered.

"After him, Judas the Galilean appeared in the days of the census and led a band of people in revolt. He too was killed, and all his followers were scattered."

The murmurs of agreement grew louder as Gamaliel paused and looked at the counsel before continuing.

"Therefore, in the present case, my advice to you is clear: Leave these men alone. Let them go! If their purpose or activity is of human origin, it will fail. But if it is from God, you will not be able to stop them. You will only find yourselves fighting against God."

"But these men deliberately disobeyed the directives of this counsel, preaching and healing in the name of their criminal leader—" objected Matthias.

"Then punish them for disobedience," Gamaliel responded, "but be careful what you do. If Jesus was truly the criminal many of you believe him to be, his followers will soon fade into obscurity without the need for any further involvement by this counsel."

Gamaliel's reasoning persuaded the Sanhedrin to call the apostles back in, have them flogged with a whip, order them not to speak in the name of Jesus, and let them go.

The disciples left rejoicing because they had been counted worthy of suffering for their Lord and Master. Day after day, in the temple courts and from house to house, they never stopped teaching and proclaiming the good news that Jesus is the Messiah sent by God to redeem the world, that God had ushered in a new and better covenant, and that those who placed their faith and trust in God's Messiah would have an everlasting relationship with God.

Their determination did not fade, and their efforts in spreading Jesus' message produced results far more widespread and long lasting than they could have ever imagined. They were persecuted for the message they proclaimed—but the persecution merely caused the word to be spread wider and to a greater audience.

Even those persecuting the "Christians"—as they came to be known—noted that they were turning the world upside down for their Christ and their redeemer. They were literally following their Lord's great commission to go into all the world and preach the good news of God's love, grace and salvation to all they met.

*****

Even today, committed followers of Christ continue to make disciples of men and women by proclaiming the message Jesus told Nicodemus approximately two thousand years ago—that God loves the world so much that he gave his one and only Son, that whoever believes in him should not perish, but rather will have eternal life.

About the Author

Although Bill Kincaid spent over 35 years practicing law in Texas, he started out as a writer and journalist. He was sports editor and political editor for his high school paper, edited his university newspaper, and worked for several Texas newspapers before earning his doctor of jurisprudence degree from Texas Tech University's School of Law. Several of his articles and columns received state-wide honors.

Now that Kincaid is slowing down his legal practice, he finally has time to return to his writing roots, publishing two books in 2013 that are almost as different from each other as day is from night.

Nicodemus' Quest is a Christian historical fiction novel that makes as much use of Kincaid's ability to do detailed research as it does of his ability to tell a good story. *The Baptist Standard* called the book "a compelling, inventive, moving novel . . . a great story" and said that "extensive biblical, historical, geographical, archeological, and linguistic research exudes from each page."

On the other hand, *Ronald Raygun and the Sweeping Beauty* is a fractured fairy tale that satirizes such well known stories as *Sleeping Beauty, The Princess and the Pea,* and *Cinderella.* What makes the story even more fun is the humor that is woven throughout, not to mention various political references that permeate the work. Some are obvious (such as in the title), but most are extremely subtle and unobtrusive.

Kincaid is continuing to write on varied topics. In 2014, he published *Saul's Quest,* a novel about the Apostle Paul's life through his first missionary journey. Wizard's Gambit, his first science fiction fantasy, is scheduled to be published in 2015.

He and his wife, Audette, have been married for more than 40 years and have three adult children, Cheryl-Annette, Christina, and Sharlene.

221

46213949R00123

Made in the USA
Charleston, SC
13 September 2015